He was every bit the tyrant she expected

Slamming the door, Burke relentlessly backed her against the wall, a hand on each side of her. An odd brooding look passed over his face. "I wonder why you insist on challenging me."

Susan forced herself to look steadily into his fierce gray eyes. "I just don't think you're an all-seeing god who knows what's best for everyone else."

"I think it's something more basic than that," Burke said. "You're a lady who's just looking for a man to master her."

"Do you really think I'd be interested in a big bad cowboy who thinks he can throw his weight around?"

"Let's find out, shall we?" His hand encircled her neck while his head descended with lightning speed. Expecting harshness, she was disarmed by his lips, soft and caressing. She could feel herself responding. . . .

Jeanne Allan, born and raised in Nebraska, lived there until she married a United States Air Force lieutenant. More than a dozen moves have taken them to Germany and ten different states. Between moves Jeanne spends time as a seasoned volunteer, and makes all kinds of crafts including stained-glass windows. With their two teenage children, she enjoys nature walks, bird-watching and photography at their cabin in the Colorado mountains. She has always liked to write, but says her husband bullied her into writing her first romance novel.

The Waiting Heart

Jeanne Allan

Harlequin Books

TORONTO • NEW YORK • LONDON
AMSTERDAM • PARIS • SYDNEY • HAMBURG
STOCKHOLM • ATHENS • TOKYO • MILAN

Original hardcover edition published in 1986
by Mills & Boon Limited

ISBN 0-373-02875-X

Harlequin Romance first edition December 1987

CHAPTER ONE

THE brisk December wind blowing up white plumes from the snowy patches that dotted the Colorado landscape made Susan thankful for the warmth spilling from her car's heater. A grey haze to the west hid the Rocky Mountains from her view, but she knew they towered there, abrupt and powerful . . . and arrogant. Strange that such an odd description occurred to her. She had never thought of the Rockies as arrogant before. Beautiful and exciting, even rugged, yes, but arrogant? Instinctively she knew that once again her subconscious thoughts had drifted to her upcoming meeting with Burke Gerard. Disturbing memories of a commanding voice ringing over the telephone lines sent a deep shiver through Susan's slender body. She was crazy to have accepted Elizabeth's invitation to spend the holidays at the Gerard ranch.

As if to suit her mood, the day darkened, and snow began to fall heavily. She had dismissed the occasional white flake drifting by earlier as of no consequence, but this snow had the makings of a real storm. Switching on her headlights helped little. The huge white flakes took on a threatening air as they thickened and swirled about the car, sticking to the windscreen wipers in ominous clumps. Susan uttered a few unladylike words as she gripped the steering wheel with nervous intensity. It was one thing to drive city streets, sanded and well-ploughed by

maintenance crews, and quite another to drive
unfamiliar country roads where she hadn't passed
another car since turning off from the main highway
fifteen minutes earlier. She crept along, searching in
vain for the turn-off to the Gerard ranch. Elizabeth
had said it would be easy to spot, being marked with
a large grey mailbox. On a sunny day that might be
true, but the mailbox would blend in remarkably well
with the present grey skies. Just then her headlights
picked out a familiar shape, and pulling to the side of
the road, Susan rolled down her car window and
brushed the snow from the box with a gloved hand.
A sigh of relief escaped her at the sight of the black
letters boldly spelling out 'Gerard'.

Shivering from the cold, Susan rolled up her
window and cautiously turned into the side road.
Anxious to reach the ranch before the snow further
intensified, she recklessly pressed on the accelerator.
By the time her eyes had flashed the message to her
brain that there was a truck in her path, she was too
stunned to think. Instinctively her right foot
stamped down hard on the brake pedal. Tyres with
snow-packed treads lost their tenuous grip on the
snow-slick road. Every tip that Susan had ever read
about coming out of a skid fled her mind at the blast
of a horn and the sight of the truck headed straight
for her. In panic she pressed harder on the brakes,
putting a stop to any efforts of her car to come out of
the skid. The other driver fought with his wheel in a
futile effort to evade her car. The screech of the
impact tore at Susan's ears, and the world spun in a
crazy collage of white. The crash threw her against
the restraining belt seat as her car spun off the road
to land with a crunching thud against a very solid

boulder. She rested her head against the steering wheel, her body shaking with shock in the aftermath of the accident.

Suddenly her car door was wrenched open, and a male voice demanded, 'What the hell do you think you're doing, shooting around the curve like that?'

Guiltily aware that the fault was hers, and still shaken by the accident, Susan merely shuddered. A harsh curse hung in the dusky air as a large form blotted out the lingering rays of the sun which entered the car. Susan's head was gently tipped back against the seat while two large hands swiftly and impersonally examined her body. She opened her eyes to protest at the intimate search, but her indignation died away as she looked directly into penetrating grey eyes, deep set under a furrowed brow. The face was somehow familiar: tanned, rugged, taut with concern. A thatch of sunbleached hair, which had escaped from the parka hood covering the man's head, was dotted with flakes of snow. She closed her eyes to escape from his intense scrutiny and fought off the wave of weakness that washed over her.

'Now is no time to faint, lady.' The deep voice grated on her ears.

'I have no intention of fainting.' She was pleased that her own voice sounded strong and clear. Willing her fingers not to tremble, she struggled to undo the seat belt.

Impatient hands thrust hers aside, and the belt was quickly disposed of. Strong arms pulled her from the driver's seat. 'I don't think there's anything broken—not that you deserve to come out of this unscathed! Anyone who drives that fast on roads like this . . . And then to hit your brakes, which you obviously did. My God, the rankest amateur knows to steer into a skid instead of trying to get out of it!'

Any thoughts that Susan might have had about apologising fled instantly. 'So, sue me,' she flashed. Couldn't this brute see how shaken she was by what had happened? If that wasn't just like one of her brothers, to stand there and rage instead of trying to do something about the situation.

'I ought to wring your pretty little neck,' he returned, surveying the results of the crash with a disgusted air.

Susan leaned against the front bumper of her car. Her legs wobbled and threatened to fold at any minute. For the first time she looked about and realised the total extent of the accident. Her car was totally off the road, tilted at a crazy angle with the boot firmly wedged against a large boulder. The beam of its headlights reflected off snowflakes falling from the sky in ever-increasing numbers. In the opposite ditch a dark pick-up truck rested nose down, a back wheel spinning slowly in the air.

A restless movement at her side brought Susan's attention back to the man beside her. It was darker now, and harder to make out his face. A faint memory tugged at her mind, but she knew she had never met him. Impossible to forget a man like this! The heavy parka served to camouflage him to some extent, but there was no hiding the massive shoulders and extreme height. Masculinity and power emanated from the dark figure, and Susan suddenly remembered that she was alone with this stranger on a country road, with night falling. She edged away.

'We'll have to walk.'

The pronouncement caught her off guard. 'Walk? I'm not going anywhere with you!' she said shrilly.

'Now what? Let me guess: hysterics.' He reached in her car, turned off the headlights and removed her keys before shutting the door.

'Give me those,' she demanded, backing away as he turned in her direction. With an exaggerated sigh he dropped the keys into her outstretched hand. She struggled to reopen her car door with hands stiffened from the cold.

He ignored her efforts as he walked to his pick-up, and turned off its lights. Looking over his shoulder, he addressed her, 'You'll need something warmer to wear. It's almost two miles to the ranch.'

'You obviously weren't listening. I'm not going to any ranch.'

'If you weren't going to the ranch, why were you driving hell for leather on this road?' His tone was that of an adult trying to reason with a recalcitrant child.

'I wasn't driving hell for leather,' Susan asserted hotly. Even in the growing dark she caught his sarcastic glance. 'All right,' she conceded. 'Maybe I was going a little faster than the conditions warranted. How was I to know that you would come speeding towards me?'

'Oh, no. You can't blame the accident on me.' He slammed shut the pick-up door.

Hastily Susan renewed her efforts on the door handle as he moved towards her. 'A typical male chauvinistic attitude,' she retorted. 'Always blame a woman for your troubles.' She finally wrested open the car door. 'You can stand around and whine all you want, but I have no intention of doing so.' Long experience with her brothers had taught her that her best defence was to put them in the wrong.

This man was made of stronger stuff. He leaned against the front bumper of her car, crossed long booted legs, and drawled, 'Just what *are* your plans, lady?'

Fully intending to show him that she was not the naïve driver that he thought her, she grabbed the floor mats and placed one under each rear tyre. Ignoring the look of derision on his face, she got in the car and turned on the engine. The motor obligingly coughed to life, but the car refused to move. She tried to reverse but only succeeded in grinding the rear end of the car deeper against the boulder. Annoyed, she put the car in first gear again and floor-boarded the accelerator. The car whined in protest but refused to budge.

The man yanked open the car door, and reaching in, turned off the engine and pocketed her keys. 'You're just wasting fuel. We'll need a four-wheel-drive to pull both these babies out.'

'Nonsense. Give me back my keys, and you can push while I try again.'

'Don't you ever listen, lady? I said it won't work.'

'And are you always the final authority on matters?'

'I am around here. I own this place. My name is Burke Gerard,' he added.

Of course, Susan thought with resignation. Belatedly she recognised the resemblance to Randy that had teased at her. How could she ever have forgotten this man's hard, sarcastic voice? The accident must have rattled her more than she'd realised.

'I should have known. The great man himself. Too important to his business to spend time with mere mortals, even his own mother. Your arrogance should have identified you for me immediately!'

Burke Gerard said nothing for a moment, squinting down at her through narrowed lids. 'And I should have recognised you by your caustic tongue, not to mention misplaced courage in rushing in where angels fear to tread, not that I think you're any angel, Miss Osborne,' he drawled insultingly. Leaning into the car, he grasped her chin with a firm hand and forced it up for his careful scrutiny. 'Well, well, Elizabeth's schoolteacher come to call! What a delightful surprise!'

Susan matched him, stare for stare. She realised that if this man discerned the trembling beneath her cool exterior, he would instantly pounce on her weakness. 'My arrival will be no surprise to Elizabeth. She's expecting me.'

'So she is,' he muttered. 'And what is little Miss Carrie Nation going to crusade about this time?' he asked in a jeering voice.

'I don't know what you mean,' she answered coldly.

'Sure you do. You're just itching to get to the ranch and set us all straight on our duties and responsibilities.'

'If the shoe fits . . .' Susan flared.

'Oh, it doesn't fit, teacher, but you never bothered to find that out, did you? It must be wonderful to know what everyone else should do. Is that why you're a teacher? Because you like to tell people what to do?'

'Me? You're the overbearing bully who's always yelling out orders!'

'At least I'm not an officious busybody.'

'Busybody!' she shrieked, glaring up at him as he stood stiffly beside her. Breathing deeply, she forced herself to calm down. Now was not the time to let this man rattle her with his unfounded accusations intended to put her in the wrong instead of himself. 'I can't see that all this name-calling is getting us anywhere. We'd better decide what we're going to do.'

Burke Gerards's lips tightened at her patient, reasonable tone, and she flinched when he reached towards her, but he was only shoving her away from the open car door. His eyes glinted at her sudden movement before he leaned inside the car. 'Where's your coat?'

Susan blinked at the unexpected question before glancing down at the fashionable waistcoat and sweater that she had thrown on earlier in the day. Bright blue skies this morning when she was packing had given no indication that the weather was planning a drastic turn for the worse. 'It's in the back,' she admitted with a guilty glance at the clearly inaccessible boot.

'Oh fine. Along with your hat and boots, I suppose,' he said, disgust at her stupidity coating his words.

'I could hardly have known when I set out that I might need to take a winter hike, could I?' she returned heatedly.

'This is Colorado, teacher. You should always be prepared.'

'Quit calling me teacher! My name is Susan.' She

refused to admit that her landlady had reminded her only this morning how quickly Colorado weather could change. Moving away from the car and from Burke Gerard showed Susan too late how both had sheltered her from the rising wind. Her bulky-knit sweater provided scant protection from the biting cold, and she could not control her shivering.

Heaving a loud sigh of irritation, Burke tramped over to the pick-up. From the dark depths he pulled something out and handed it to her, commanding tersely, 'Wear this.'

Taking the navy watch cap that he held out, Susan gingerly perched it on her head, wrinkling her nose in distaste at the smoky odour that clung to it. Without a word, Burke reached over and yanked the cap firmly down over her ears. She opened her mouth to protest, met his challenging gaze, and swallowed her words. This man was quite capable of abandoning her.

'Very wise, teacher,' he breathed. Reaching into the truck's cab again, he pulled out a dirty plaid blanket which Susan suspected normally covered a horse. One sniff confirmed her suspicions. However, the blanket, draped over her shoulders, did block out the biting cold, so she resolutely endeavoured to ignore the smell. Burke took one look at her face and burst out laughing. 'I suppose it does smell pretty strong to a city girl!'

Susan couldn't answer. The change in Burke's face when he laughed had rocked her back on her heels. Here was a charm that his normal brusque manner concealed very well. What a shame he didn't do it more often. Too late she realised that Burke had turned and walked away again.

'Where are you going?' she enquired.

'I told you: we'll have to walk to the ranch. It's a couple of miles from here, so the sooner we get going, the better. We've already wasted enough time here.' A sideways look left Susan in no doubt as to whom Burke was blaming for the wasted time.

She shivered at the idea of walking so far in the cold and growing darkness. 'Why can't we just wait for someone to come after us? After all, I'm expected. Surely someone will come looking for me.'

'Don't count on it. You wouldn't let Randy bring you because you said that you weren't sure when you could get away. What was it? Another date, only it didn't work out, so here you are?'

Susan barely heard his last words, a sinking feeling invading her stomach as she admitted to herself the truth of his first ones. She had indeed refused Randy's offer of a ride. Mentally she cursed the brothers whose cosseting care had engendered in her a wilful independence. The truth was, she didn't come with Randy because she wanted to have her own car so she could be free to come and go as she pleased. Since she didn't want to hurt Randy by telling him that, she had used the excuse of a mythical teachers' meeting. She looked up at Burke, standing impatiently beside her. 'What about you?'

'In case it escaped your notice, I was headed the other way when you rammed me. I won't be expected back for hours.'

'Oh.' She was darned if she would apologise to him for ruining his date. Whoever the woman was, she ought to thank Susan for a timely rescue.

Burke didn't seem to expect any other comment from her. No doubt he thought that he had at last browbeaten her into submission as he gave her a small shove down the road.

Suddenly Susan didn't want to leave the security of her car. She was cold, she was tired, and the thought of walking two miles in falling snow on an unfamiliar road beside this cold stranger was more than she could cope with. What if Burke walked so fast she couldn't keep up with him? He was just the type to walk off and abandon her. She wouldn't go with him; Elizabeth would send someone back for her.

'I'm staying here,' she announced as firmly as she could through chattering teeth. 'Someone can drive back and get me.'

Burke impatiently turned to her, started to say something, and then merely shrugged and began walking back in the direction of his tyre tracks. As his body grew smaller in the distance Susan felt more and more alone. One lonely star popped out in the sky above her, mocking her decision. She'd go and wait in her car. As she started towards it, a pile of leaves, brushed bare of snow by the wind, rustled and moved. Susan stopped in panic. Surely that was only the wind? Never having lived in the country, she could only imagine the creatures that might be loose on a night like this. She had to pass the leaves to get to her car, but her legs refused to budge. Frantically she looked down the road. Burke was a tiny figure in the distance. Wrestling with the flapping ends of the blanket, she ran after him, hoarsely crying out his name. At last he heard her cries and turned, hands on hips, to watch her ungainly approach.

'Change your mind about waiting?' he asked sarcastically.

Her lungs were searing from running in the cold air. She gasped for breath and struggled for dignity. 'I decided it wasn't right to expect anyone to make an extra trip,' she managed eventually.

The look of disbelief on Burke's face told her that he saw right through her subterfuge, but he made no comment, merely waiting impatiently until she had regained her breath, and then he ploughed on without even looking to see if she were following. His attitude was almost enough to send Susan scurrying back to her car, until she remembered the disturbing rustle of leaves.

They walked along in silence, Susan plodding several paces behind Burke. Resentfully she eyed his back and his easy-going stride. For him this was nothing more than an evening stroll, while she was uneasily aware that she would not be able to keep up this quick pace for the entire distance. Anyone else would have realised that, but not this man, she thought bitterly, glaring at Burke striding even further ahead of her. Her own previous contact with him no doubt exemplified how he bullied his way through life expecting—no, demanding—that everyone else do his bidding. Months had passed, but Susan had neither forgiven nor forgotten Burke Gerard's arrogant treatment of her.

Night had completely fallen, but at least the snow was easing up. The drifting flakes brought back a rush of memories. Although nominally spring, the night she had met Elizabeth had been much like this. After a shopping excursion at the huge Aurora Mall late one afternoon, Susan had been surprised to see snow coming lightly down as she had walked back to her car. Two people struggling in the deserted car park caught her attention. She could still remember the sick fear that had swept through her body when she'd heard a woman scream and realised that she was the only person near enough to be aware of the woman's plight. Yelling loudly herself, she had rushed to the woman's aid, fortunately scaring off the assailant, who was little more than a teenager. Susan had felt ill all over again when she had spotted the knife that the boy had dropped in his rush to get away, but one look at the elderly lady lying on the ground had convinced her that she had no time for any weakness. Two other teenage boys, arriving in time to see the mugger flee, had given chase, and although they lost the boy in the growing darkness, they did stumble over the bag that he had tossed aside. Returning to Susan's aid, they promptly called the police and an ambulance. By this time, the woman, who had identified herself as Elizabeth Gerard, was in extreme pain and shock, and refused to allow Susan to leave her, so Susan had accompanied her to the hospital.

While the woman was undergoing emergency surgery for what turned out to be a broken leg suffered when the mugger had flung her to the ground, Susan had remembered the bag. Reluctantly going through it, she had found Burke's name and had endeavoured to contact him, believing him to be the injured woman's husband. Unable to reach him, she had left a message with the housekeeper.

Hours passed before Burke had finally called the hospital, by which time Susan was torn between rage at his lack of concern, and worry that Elizabeth's husband was so elderly that he'd been unable to cope with the disastrous news. When the nurse had finally summoned her to the phone, the crisp, deep voice coming over the wires had immediately shattered any illusions that Susan might have had about a panicky or overwrought elderly husband. First, he had demanded to know her name, and too stunned to argue, she had told him. Next he had informed her that it would be a day or two before he could get there, so Susan was now in charge of Elizabeth. She was to make sure that Elizabeth wanted for nothing, or she, Susan, would answer to him.

Furiously Susan had lashed out that she was a stranger and had asked what kind of monster was he that he couldn't even come to visit his wife in the hospital. A short silence had greeted her outburst, and then the voice had informed her coldly that Elizabeth was his mother, and that he was in the middle of a blizzard, and unless she intended that he ski to Denver, he was stuck where he was for the time being. Icy contempt had roughened his voice when he'd added that if she were angling for payment, yes, he'd be happy to make it worth her while to watch over his mother until he could reach Denver and take over.

The tensions of the past few hours had built up in Susan to an unbearable pitch, and Burke's crude insinuations had been like a match to dry tinder. In an explosive rage that had later shamed her, she'd given Burke her opinions on his lack of concern for his mother, his lack of responsibility in caring for her, and his lack of gratitude to Susan, not to mention his insult to her. She had been in full cry on exactly what he could do with his ranch, his cows and his blizzard when he had cut sharply into her diatribe, saying angrily that he would be there as soon as possible and that she had damn well better be present at his mother's bedside when he did get there. Before she could react to his outrageous directive, he'd hung up, leaving her fuming at the other end of the line.

Burke had been bossy, arrogant, self-centred and a bully. Tonight proved that was his normal behaviour. Dark thoughts concerning his come-uppance at her hands gave her the strength to plod on in his footsteps. Head bowed against the slight wind, she could feel the moisture creeping in through the thin soles of her shoes, while her fingers clutching the blanket were growing numb with cold. Head down, she failed to see the substantial bulk in her path until she ploughed into Burke's hard body. His arms instinctively enfolded her as she lost her balance. The instant shelter from the wind felt heavenly, and Susan leaned thankfully against his solid warmth.

Burke said something, but the wind carried away his words, and she looked up with a questioning air. He leaned down and tugged the cap away from her ear. 'I said, we're over half way now.'

'Only half way?' Susan replied faintly. 'It seems like we've been walking for ever.'

Burke frowned down at her. 'I suppose you're going to tell me you can't make it,' he said, his tone of voice leaving no doubt in Susan's mind that he considered her a weakling.

She stiffened and stepped back from his shielding arms. 'Of course I can.'

Burke merely raised a sceptical eyebrow and started off again. Not having the extra breath to bandy words with him, Susan saved her strength to move her weary body down the seemingly endless road. To her relief Burke slowed down his pace, but she refused to thank him. Muttering under her breath, she ploughed ahead. She would die before she would give him the satisfaction of seeing her collapse at his feet. In an effort to take her mind off her present discomfort, Susan deliberately turned her thoughts to Burke's arrogant and ungenerous conduct at the time of his mother's mishap.

If Burke had shown up at Elizabeth's bedside shortly thereafter, Susan might have been able to forgive his behaviour, reasoning that hearing of his mother's injury would upset any man. As it was, Elizabeth's younger son, Randy, was the first to arrive. Summoned by his older brother, he arrived as soon as the roads from Fort Collins, where he attended the university, were cleared. After visiting his mother, he had offered to go down to the ranch to help Burke out, an offer his older brother had declined, no doubt to avoid leaving Elizabeth in Susan's predatory hands. Elizabeth had scotched that idea by insisting that she was perfectly all right and sending Randy back to his studies, secure in the knowledge that Burke would be arriving shortly.

It was a woebegone Elizabeth who had greeted Susan the following evening. Once again Burke had telephoned his excuses for not coming to the hospital. Elizabeth had professed to understand, but Susan had been enraged at the man's neglect of his mother. Making an excuse to leave Elizabeth for a few minutes, Susan had hurried to a pay phone and called Burke once more. This time she had immediately laid in to him for neglecting his mother. He had been furious, calling her a smug, interfering, officious busybody, among other names not so nice.

She had called him arrogant, callous and heartless. Battle was enjoined, and it wasn't until Susan noticed the significant looks from the nurses' station that she realised how loudly she was shouting. Without a further word to Burke she had slammed down the receiver, abruptly terminating the conversation. It had taken her fifteen minutes to cool down to the point where she could return to Elizabeth's room without informing the patient that her number one son was a boorish oaf who didn't care two beans for his mother.

The next afternoon a radiant Elizabeth announced that Burke had been to the hospital that morning to visit her, and that he was returning that evening. She wanted Susan to stay and meet him. Susan, remembering Burke's harsh indictment of her and the awful accusations she'd made, had immediately recalled a non-existent meeting and had left the hospital before Burke's anticipated arrival. That set the pattern for the remainder of Elizabeth's hospital stay. Burke apparently had as little wish to encounter Susan as she did to meet him, for he was always careful to inform Elizabeth in advance of his visiting plans, and Susan was just as careful to make certain that their visits did not coincide.

Belatedly aware that her emotions had overruled her good sense, Susan had never mentioned that second phone call to Elizabeth, and apparently, neither had Burke. It never failed to amaze Susan that a woman as sweet and generous as Elizabeth could have raised such a selfish son as Burke. Even stranger was the fact that Elizabeth appeared to be totally oblivious to her elder son's faults. And as much as Susan would relish the idea of putting Burke firmly in his place, a warm and unexpected friendship was growing between the two women, despite their disparate interests, and Susan had no wish to jeopardise that embryonic friendship.

Which made this visit all the sillier. If Elizabeth hadn't called with the invitation just as Susan had finished reading a letter from her older brother Tom that had left her feeling like Orphan Annie, she would never have succumbed to Elizabeth's pleadings. A moment's thought would have reminded her that she was lucky her brothers were both oceans away from running her life. If she had really been dispirited at the thought of spending Christmas alone, she had other friends. They would have invited her to share their plans, and in fact did. Only by then she was committed to Elizabeth. Committed and not knowing how to get out of it.

Cautious enquiry had put paid to any hopes that Elizabeth's sons wouldn't be home for Christmas. Not that she minded Randy, Elizabeth's younger son. She had met him many times at the hospital, and found him friendly as a young puppy. Again she wondered how it was that Elizabeth had managed to give birth to two such total opposites. Seeing Randy at the hospital, Susan had been warmed by the care and consideration that he had shown his mother. Business and monetary interests would never interfere to keep him from Elizabeth's side if she needed him. Randy would never delegate the care of his mother to a perfect stranger much as he would dictate a letter to a secretary.

Susan's lip curled in scorn. Just thinking about how Burke had ignored his mother's welfare and how patient and understanding Elizabeth had been about his cavalier behaviour still made her blood boil. And ordering her around, a total stranger! The man deserved to be shot.

Pulling the blanket more snugly about her to discourage the flow of cold air, Susan concentrated on putting one foot in front of the other. Some other time she might have appreciated the beauty of the clear winter night with the snow glistening in the moonlight, but right now all she wanted was a hot bath. The cold air tore at her exposed face, causing her eyes to water and her nose to run.

Burke gave a grunt of satisfaction, and involuntarily she looked up at him. 'What is it?'

'Do you see the glow ahead of us on the horizon?' he asked.

She nodded, and then, realising he might not be able to make out her answer in the dark, managed a breathless assent.

'That's from the lights at the ranch.' He looked down at her. 'Not much farther now. Just over this last little hill.'

'Little?' cried Susan, looking at the hill ahead of her. 'It looks like Mount Everest to me!'

Burke chuckled as he strode ahead. Susan was sure that she'd never heard such a heartless sound in her entire life. Sniffing audibly, she trudged on in his wake. A hole in the road caught her completely off guard and, yelping in surprise, she tumbled to the snowy ground.

At her cry, Burke halted and returned quickly to her side. 'Don't you ever look where you're going?' he asked in exasperation.

Disdaining his extended hand, Susan struggled to her feet. Burke reached over to brush the clinging

snow from her, and she slapped away his hands.
'Leave me alone!' she cried, near her breaking point.
After the accident, walking for ever in the cold and
dark, and falling, it was just too much to endure
Burke's snarling at her again. Why had she come?
Even if she had to spend the entire Christmas
holiday totally alone, that was better than being
around such an arrogant beast even for one second.

Once again, in defiance of the elements, Burke
surged ahead. Indignation speeded up Susan's own
steps, but soon the numbing cold slowed her back
down to a stumbling pace. Her head sunk deep on to
her chest, she trudged on, oblivious to her surroundings, aware only of the intense cold, until once again
something in her path tripped her up. This time,
Burke reacted quickly, and a strong arm held her
upright. Susan was too exhausted to deny that she
needed his help. Wearily she leaned against his
shoulder. If she could only rest!

CHAPTER TWO

IT took a moment before Susan understood the words that Burke kept repeating in her ear. Finally they sank through her apathy, and she looked up to see light streaming through the small panes of a door in front of her. She had tripped over porch stairs. Galvanised by the welcome light, she eagerly forced her weary legs up the steps, uncaring that Burke's solid arm was helping her.

Before they reached the door, it swung open, light and heat flooding out into the cold night to embrace her. Elizabeth stood in the open doorway peering out into the darkness. 'Is that you, Susan?' Someone unseen switched on an outside light. 'Burke, what are you doing back here?'

Burke hustled Susan into a large entry hall before turning to answer his mother's surprised enquiry. 'You might say Susan and I unexpectedly ran into each other,' he explained drily. He went on to sketch briefly the details of their accident. To Susan's surprise, no mention was made of her disastrous driving, Burke merely blaming the mishap on the weather and the icy roads. Tired from the unexpected hike and bone-chilling cold, she was content to let him do all the explaining as she stood wearily in the hall. Catching sight of herself in a large ornate mirror hanging nearby, she couldn't decide whether to laugh or cry. Wet tendrils of blonde hair clung limply to her face beneath the shapeless dark hat.

25

Her face was red and pinched from cold, while her eyes and nose were suspiciously moist. Seen in the light, the pungent plaid blanket showed definite signs of its purpose, and Susan could see short horse hairs stuck to her damp face and neck.

The sound of her name distracted her attention from the unappealing image in the mirror. Elizabeth, concern etched on her kindly face, was talking to her. 'Why don't you head straight for the bathroom and take a hot bath? You must be absolutely frozen! I should have sent one of the men out to look for you earlier,' she fussed, taking the blanket from Susan's numb fingers with a grimace on her face. 'Goodness, Burke, is that the best you could do? This smells terrible!' she scolded.

'Keeping Susan warm was my primary concern,' he returned casually, shaking out of his outer garments, as oblivious to the snow and water dripping from his clothes as he was to the matronly dark-haired lady who scolded his carelessness as she wiped up the floor.

Ignoring his implication that her own stupidity was responsible for the necessity of wearing the blanket, Susan turned gratefully to Elizabeth. 'A bath sounds wonderful. Just point me to the bathroom, and I can fix it.'

'Nonsense; I'll help you. Where are your things?'

'I'm afraid I had to leave my suitcase behind.'

'Oh dear,' Elizabeth said in distress. 'Burke, surely you could have . . .'

'No, I couldn't have,' he denied firmly. 'Did you expect me to carry all her luggage two miles in the snow? Someone can get her things in the morning,' he added brusquely as he disappeared down the hall.

Even Elizabeth seemed disconcerted by Burke's behaviour, but she rallied quickly, offering to lend her what she needed.

Only a few minutes elapsed before Susan was laying her head back against the bath's rim, letting the warmth of the water seep through her body. Elizabeth had been generous with the bath salts, and the soft, scented water lapped under her chin as she wearily closed her eyes. Not a good beginning to a visit she wished she had refused. Burke couldn't have made it clearer that he didn't welcome her presence. Any other man would have been grateful to her for caring for his mother, but not Burke. He had neither forgotten nor forgiven what he called her unwarranted interference. That was just too bad; under the same circumstances she would do it again in a flash. All that nonsense about blizzards and responsibilities. A son should hire people to take care of his cows, not his mother. Burke Gerard had needed a little shaking up to show him where his priorities should be. If he chose to dislike her for it— well, it was often the fate of the messenger to be cursed along with the message.

In spite of her philosophical rationalisation, Susan shuddered to remember the cold look in Burke's eyes when he had realised who she was. Blaming her sudden chill on a cooling bath, she turned on the hot tap. Elizabeth would soon be up to see if she had drowned, she thought drowsily. On the heels of that thought the bathroom door opposite the one she had entered through opened, and Burke walked into the bathroom. Furiously Susan sat up. The immediate gleam in Burke's eye drove her back under the bubbles. 'What do you think you're doing? Get out of my bathroom!'

One sleek eyebrow, arched in sardonic amusement, betrayed Burke's feelings as he slowly exited from the room, closing the door behind him with exaggerated care. 'The point is,' the deceptively mild words came from the other side of the door, 'it's not your bathroom; it's mine. And you've been tying it up for the better part of an hour now. You're not the only one who was unexpectedly stranded in the snow,' he added, the emphasis on the word 'unexpectedly' to convey to Susan that no matter what he had said to the others, he blamed her for their accident.

Belatedly remembering that Elizabeth had mentioned that Susan's bedroom shared access to the bathroom with Burke's, even Burke's implied nasty crack about her driving failed to penetrate Susan's embarrassment. How could she have blithely sat in the bath so long without first locking Burke's door? The memory of the gleam in Burke's eyes lent ice to her voice as she assured him that she was almost through.

'Let's hope so. Because you have only five minutes to get out of that tub. Then I'm coming back in there to take a shower whether you're still there or not.'

'You wouldn't!' cried Susan.

'No? Is that a dare?' There was a disturbing tone to his words, half threat and half amusement.

'I'm not daring you,' she snapped. 'I said I'd be out in a couple of minutes, and I will.'

'Too bad.' He was definitely amused now. 'I kind of liked the sneak preview you showed me.'

Fuming ineffectively, Susan viciously squeezed her wet, soapy sponge, wishing it were Burke's neck.

Of all the rude, infuriating males!

A short time later, sitting in bed and wrapped in a voluminous flannel robe belonging to Elizabeth, Susan pushed the tray away from her legs. 'That soup was ambrosia from heaven! I didn't realise how hungry I was. I apologise for putting you to all this trouble.'

'It's no trouble, Susan. I'm just happy that there were no serious consequences to your accident.'

Susan twisted the bedspread between nervous fingers before looking straight at Elizabeth. 'I'm afraid that the accident was all my fault. I was going too fast, and reacted in all the wrong ways. I'll pay, of course, for any damages to Burke's pick-up.'

'That's not necessary.' Elizabeth's voice was brisk as she removed the supper tray to a nearby table. 'Burke told me that he couldn't see any damage to the truck—that both vehicles landed in drifted snow. His only concern is that you may have put a dent in the back of your car.'

'He probably thinks it serves me right,' retorted Susan.

'I get the impression that you and Burke didn't exactly hit it off,' Elizabeth prodded.

Susan smiled ruefully at the older woman. 'Running a man into a ditch isn't exactly the way to his heart.'

Elizabeth laughed. 'No, I suppose it isn't. But you two appeared as prickly as porcupines when you walked in the front door. It was obvious you'd been having words.'

'Elizabeth, I had just walked two miles. I was too tired to have words with anyone. What are our plans for the holidays?' she pointedly changed the subject.

'Oh no, you don't, young lady, I'm not that easily put off. Was Burke terribly rude about the accident?'

'Wouldn't you be?' countered Susan.

'Burke is as susceptible to a pretty face as the next man. Surely after you apologised . . .' Elizabeth's voice trailed off at the stubborn look on Susan's face. 'I see,' she said drily. 'No apology.'

'Apologise to someone as arrogant and bullying as Burke? You must be kidding. Why, he's the most conceited, self-centred . . .' Her tirade ground to a halt as she belatedly remembered that the man she was lambasting was Elizabeth's son. 'I guess he did sort of put my back up,' she finished weakly.

Elizabeth laughed. 'He does have his bossy moments, but after you get to know him, you'll find he's not all that bad.'

'You could be right,' Susan conceded reluctantly. 'It's just that after my brothers, I'm allergic to any male who comes on like Tarzan.'

'Like Tarzan?' asked Elizabeth blankly.

'You know—me Tarzan, you Jane. Me heap big warrior, you little woman who's too dumb to tie her shoes.'

'Susan, I can't believe you're saying that. That attitude went out with the Dark Ages.'

'Not for Burke,' Susan said darkly.

'Well, maybe sometimes he is a little autocratic,' the older woman admitted. 'But look at his background. As you know, my husband died while Burke was still in graduate school. Poor James had no idea that he wouldn't be running the ranch years from now, and he left things in a rather messy state. His business associates had no intention of allowing Burke to take his father's place. Burke had quite a battle: youth can be such a disadvantage in the world of business. Too many people tried to undermine Burke's authority, cheat him, wrest away control of the family business. Burke won out over them, but at such a cost.'

'What do you mean?'

'He was such an open, trusting person. Thrown out into the business world, he had to become old, wise and strong overnight. He built up a hard shell around himself. He has a reputation for being tough and ruthless, but he's always honest and fair. Deep inside of him is still a loving, caring person, but only to his family and a few close friends does he divulge his inner self.' Elizabeth glanced over at Susan and then continued. 'Perhaps, if he'd have married, a wife would have softened his hard edges.'

'I'm surprised that he isn't married,' said Susan, a mental picture of Burke's massive shoulders and tousled dark blond hair coming to mind.

'Actually, he was engaged once,' Elizabeth confided. 'To the daughter of a dear friend and neighbour. The two of them grew up together, and Tiffany idolised Burke. We all knew that they would eventually marry. Burke presented Tiffany with a diamond on her nineteenth birthday. Then my husband died, and Burke was caught up in managing the business and trying to cope with a multitude of unfamiliar details. The next two years were a long, constant struggle for Burke. Looking back on it now, I can see that Tiffany must have felt neglected.' Everything probably would have worked out, but then a friend of Burke's from his college days came to visit. Burke asked Steven to entertain Tiffany for him. They eloped a month later.'

'Oh, no!' Susan was appalled. 'Surely a good friend wouldn't steal away another's fiancée.'

Elizabeth shrugged. 'Steven Tallerton was the scion of a wealthy family back east, with a junior position in the old family law firm. He was charming, handsome, and used to getting what he wanted. He took one look at Tiffany, and wanted her. To his credit, I believe he loved her and made her very happy. They always appeared to be a devoted couple when they visited here.'

'They came back here to visit?' Susan's voice rose in astonishment.

'Not here, exactly. Tiffany's father still ranches nearby, and they naturally came back to visit him. There was enough talk when Tiffany jilted Burke; we could hardly add to it by refusing to socialise with them. Besides, it's difficult to stay angry with Tiffany, because ... well, just because Tiffany is Tiffany. What's more, the Senator, Tiffany's father, is a good friend, and he was hurt badly by Tiffany's actions. Sometimes it almost seemed as if Tiffany had wronged him more than Burke. Burke didn't say much when Tiffany left. He just immersed himself in his work. Of course he's seen other women since then, but I've always felt that he's never got over Tiffany.'

Susan could see that Burke's unfortunate engagement to this Tiffany might partially account for his misogynistic attitude, but that didn't excuse him being rude, overbearing, and a positive bully. It was her opinion that Elizabeth and Randy must have cosseted Burke too much after his ill-fated love affair, so that naturally it was impossible for him to find a woman who would spoil and indulge him the way that his mother and brother did. She returned her attention to Elizabeth.

'So when Tiffany asked, naturally I said yes.'

Aware that her mind had wandered, Susan apologised. 'I'm sorry. What did you say about Tiffany?'

'She's coming to stay with us over the holidays.'

'Coming here?'

'I thought I'd told you over the phone.'

'No, you said only your family would be here.'

'I guess we're all in the habit of thinking of Tiffany and Ronnie as almost family,' Elizabeth explained.

'Ronnie? I thought you said her husband's name was Steven.'

'Good heavens! I really didn't tell you, did I? Tiffany was widowed a couple of years ago. A terrible thing. Her husband was flying to upper New York with a client, and they crashed in a heavy fog. Tiffany was devastated. It wasn't until this summer that she appeared to be ready to face life again. It's been a long, hard haul for her. Ronnie is her daughter,' Elizabeth answered Susan's earlier question. 'They didn't have much of a Christmas last year, and this year Tiffany wanted to have a special one out here for Ronnie, away from their memories in New York. Plans were all made when the Senator got an invitation to go to China on an agricultural exchange. Tiffany wouldn't hear of him missing such a wonderful opportunity, and so between us we agreed that she would come here to the ranch. You'll like Tiffany, and Ronnie is a sweet, intelligent child.'

'Surely that's a little awkward?'

'Because of Burke's and Tiffany's engagement?' Elizabeth asked. 'Actually, they've continued as

friends, and Tiffany told me that Burke has been her
salvation since the tragedy. He and Tiffany's father
flew out east the minute they heard about Steve and
supported her through the funeral. Steve's parents
were so crushed themselves that they were scant
comfort to Tiffany. No,' she added slowly, 'there's no
awkwardness about this visit. In fact . . .'

'In fact?' prompted Susan.

'Just between you and me,' Elizabeth confided,
'I'm happy that Burke is getting a second chance.'

'Second chance?'

'Yes, don't you see? If Burke has been waiting all
these years to find another Tiffany, here's his second
chance to have the original. Wait until you get to
know Tiffany. She's the sweetest, gentlest person.
She couldn't hurt a flea.'

'She obviously hurt Burke,' Susan felt compelled
to point out.

'She was awfully young then.' Elizabeth was
confident. 'Burke won't let her get away this time.
She's perfect for him.'

Following Elizabeth's departure, Susan wondered
drowsily what type of woman was perfect for Burke.
One who stood up to his bullying ways, or one who
catered to his every whim? Based on her own
encounters with him, she found it difficult to believe
that he would forgive a woman who had publicly
jilted him. Probably the idea of the renewed
courtship was just a pipe dream of Elizabeth's.
Maybe she thought it was time that Burke, in his
early thirties, provided her with grandchildren. The
thought of Burke cuddling a small child on his knee
made her grin. It was easier to visualise him scolding
than comforting.

Noise from the other side of the connecting door to the bathroom reminded her of Elizabeth's apology that Susan had to share the room with Burke. The other guest-room had twin beds and Elizabeth had decided to put Tiffany and her daughter in there.

Lying through her teeth, Susan had assured Elizabeth that sharing with Burke was no problem. She didn't add that she intended to make darn sure that she locked all the doors the next time she was in there. Burke's scowling face flashed across her mind. Just knowing he was next door would probably give her nightmares. Making a face in his direction, she wiggled herself into a comfortable spot and quickly fell into a deep, dreamless sleep.

Used to waking early as she was, Susan was not surprised when she looked at the clock the next morning. She had intended to sleep late, but habit had prevailed. Still, there was no reason why she couldn't lie here for a while and enjoy the luxury of not having to rush to get ready for school.

Sinking back into the banked pillows, she gazed about the lovely room. Enormous pink cabbage roses on pale blue wallpaper climbed riotously up to reach the extra high ceiling while a crocheted cover was spread over the double mattress on an old white iron bedstead. Large, antique pieces of mahogany furniture provided dark contrast to the room's pastel décor. A white marble fireplace against one wall was laid with logs even though radiators had obviously been installed at some later date. Ruffled and flounced white curtains over lowered Venetian blinds dressed the windows, one of which had earlier proved to be a narrow door leading to a small balcony. Idly Susan contemplated getting up to see what the view from her second-storey advantage would be, but decided that could wait for more energetic moments. As for now, she would lose herself in the arms of Morpheus. That sounded very literary, she told herself with approval.

The next sound she heard was not nearly so elegant. Her stomach growled. Impossible to ignore it. She glanced again at the bedside clock; Elizabeth had said she arose early to fix breakfast for the boys. Susan grinned. Only his mother could think of Burke as a 'boy'. While it might not be stretching a point to call Randy a boy, Burke was certainly a grown man.

More protests from her stomach convinced her that it was time to get up. Stretching lazily, the first thing she saw when she crawled out of bed was her luggage just inside the bedroom door. Someone had already been down to the accident site. She spared a fleeting moment to worry about damage to her car before racing over to her bags. The wooden floors were lovely, but definitely chilly.

It didn't take long to throw on a pair of jeans and a heavy honey-coloured sweater. Crossing the room, she paused to inspect her image critically in the mirror. A small smile played across her wide, generous mouth. The tall slender woman who stared back at her was a definite improvement over the drowned rat of the previous evening. Dark eyebrows contrasted pleasingly with shoulder-length golden blonde hair, while peach colour tinted her high cheekbones. Flecks of golden brown, green and gold highlighted hazel eyes defined by sooty lashes. An urgent message from her tummy regions suggested that she admire herself some other time.

As she stepped down the bottom stair into the

entry hall, the inviting smell of coffee assailed her nostrils. Following the enticing aroma, she approached an open doorway on her left. Voices could be heard, and she headed in their direction though a darkened room set with black silhouettes of table and chairs.

Pushing her way through a swinging door, she blinked in the sudden light of a large kitchen. Burke was sitting alone at a large round oak table sipping coffee and staring out of the window, while Elizabeth, her back to Susan, was stirring something on the stove.

'Good morning,' Susan greeted them.

Leaning back in his chair, Burke coolly surveyed her over the brim of his coffee mug. 'Good morning,' he returned brusquely.

Elizabeth turned in surprise. 'Why, Susan, what are you doing up so early? I thought you intended to sleep in.'

Before Susan could answer, her stomach growled loudly, and she felt the red colour rush to her face.

A muscle twitched in Burke's cheek before he turned to Elizabeth. 'There's your answer,' he said. 'All this country air is already making your city friend hungry.'

'Well, I don't know if it's the country air, but I certainly am starved. I know I'm down awfully early, but . . .' Her stomach rumbled as if on cue. 'I don't want to disrupt your schedule.'

'You're not. Come and sit down. I made scrambled eggs, and there's plenty for three.' Elizabeth placed a blue floral plate in front of Susan and heaped it with a fluffy, golden pile, similar to that in front of Burke. For the next few minutes silence reigned over the table, broken only by requests to pass something.

Her hunger finally appeased, Susan sat back in her chair with a sigh.

'Better?' Elizabeth laughed.

'Much; I'm embarrassed at how much I ate! You'd think I'd been starving for weeks. That was delicious, Elizabeth. Let me help you with the dishes.'

'Sit and enjoy your coffee. Vera comes in later, and she cleans up the mess for me.'

Ignoring Burke's cynical glance at her offer of help, Susan looked about the kitchen. It was every woman's dream with its golden-hued wooden cupboards and shiny copper pots. What she liked best was the placement of the table in front of an immense window that was framed on the outside by two enormous pine trees. A sudden movement caught Susan's eye, and closer scrutiny disclosed a large flat tray attached to the outside window frame and filled with bird seed. Several black-capped chickadees were darting to and from the feeder, snatching up large black seeds on each trip, their distinctive cries cheery in the morning air.

Conversation behind her had ceased, and she looked around to see Elizabeth bringing over fresh coffee, while Burke was also watching the birds. She was determined to be pleasant. 'What are the birds eating?' she asked.

'Sunflower seeds. We grow them.' Burke held his empty mug out to his mother.

A large flock of greyish birds with rusty backs began pecking around on the ground beneath the feeder. 'Why don't they come up to the feeder?' Susan asked curiously.

'Snowbirds are ground feeders,' said Burke.

'Snowbirds?'

'They're really juncoes, but locally most people call them snowbirds,' Elizabeth explained.

A larger bird caught Susan's eye. 'What's that beautiful black and orange one?' The red-eyed bird scratched furiously in a small pile of leaves, then flew in a low arc to a nearby bush.

Elizabeth looked out of the window. 'A rufous-sided towhee. I have several bird books if you're interested.'

'Oh, I am,' Susan answered absently, her eye on a large bluish bird that swooped in and with a harsh squawk scattered the smaller birds. Not stopping to shell the seeds, he shoved one after another into his beak.

'That greedy fellow is a jay,' Burke informed her. Apparently he, too, was maintaining the civilities for Elizabeth's sake.

'I thought blue jays had a crest on top.'

'They do.'

'But he doesn't.'

'No, he doesn't.'

'Burke, don't tease!' His mother took pity on Susan. 'That's a scrub jay, not a blue jay. We very seldom have blue jays out this far west.'

'I didn't know that.' Susan was sorry the instant she said it, as the sardonic look on Burke's face told her that as far as he was concerned, there was a lot that she didn't know. Hastening to change the subject, she plunged ahead, 'I can't imagine how I didn't recognise you the instant I saw you. I should have seen the resemblance to Randy immediately.'

Granted, at twenty, Randy was beanpole-thin, but the dark tawny hair, the slate-coloured eyes and the well-shaped nose and chin proclaimed the relationship between the two men. It was in their personalities that the two differed radically. Randy was outgoing and boisterous, his clear grey eyes radiating trust and good humour. It was obvious that Burke eyed the world more cautiously, and his massive frame was hard-edged, announcing that here was a man who knew his worth and would fight for his values.

Elizabeth smiled fondly across the table at her elder son. 'See, I keep telling you that Randy looks just like you.'

'Please,' Burke laughingly held up a protesting hand. 'Don't tell that to Randy. He complains enough that he walks in my shadow.'

'And does he?' asked Susan curiously.

'Only in his own mind. He'll come around.'

'Come around?'

'He has some crazy idea that he has to prove himself. When he was younger he wanted to climb the tallest mountains, then he thought he'd be a rodeo champion. Now he's talking about joining the Peace Corps or some such nonsense.'

'Why is it nonsense?'

'There's plenty for him to do around here. He doesn't need to run off to Africa or Asia for meaningful work.'

'Give him time,' suggested Elizabeth. 'He's still young and uncertain of what his plans are.'

'Do you want him rushing off to deepest Africa?'

'No, of course not. But I don't want to push him

into something that he doesn't want, either.'

'I was pushed, and it did me no harm.'

'That's true, but I still feel badly that your future was determined by circumstances outside your control. Sometimes I think . . .'

Burke abruptly interrupted his mother. 'I'm not complaining. I just want to do what's best for Randy.'

Susan had heard that said to her over and over again when her brothers had disagreed with any of her plans, and it still made her angry. Without stopping to think, she spoke up. 'It seems to me that Randy would be the best judge of what's best for him!'

'You've been here less than twenty-four hours, and already you're telling me how to run my family!' Burke glared at her.

'I am not! I'm merely trying to suggest that a man of twenty should be allowed to decide his own career and not be forced into something he doesn't want.'

'He's just a boy. How does he know what he wants? I was only twenty-two when Dad died. I had no intention of taking over the ranch for years.'

'And since you didn't get to do what you wanted to do, why should Randy, is that it?'

Burke threw down his napkin before answering in a cold, tight voice. 'I'm not taking out my frustrations on my brother, if that's what you're insinuating. What I've done over the past few years has been damned hard work, but at the same time it's been an exhilarating challenge. That's my whole point. Circumstances pushed me into growing up and doing a man's work, and it was good for me. It would be good for Randy, too.'

'Just because things worked out for you is no sign that they'll work out for Randy.' Susan emphatically set her coffee mug on the table as she tried to convince Burke of his wrong-headed thinking. 'I ought to know. I have two brothers who've dedicated their lives to making my decisions for me.'

'Regardless of your vast experience, I think I'll deal with my brother as I see fit,' he answered smoothly, his blue eyes glinting across the table.

The edge to his voice should have warned her, but Susan had firm convictions on the subject of interfering brothers, no matter how well-intentioned, and she was not to be dissuaded from airing them. 'If you leave Randy to make his own choices, he'll always respect your judgment. But if you insist on deciding his life for him, believe me, you'll only end up alienating him.'

Burke threw down his napkin and stood up. 'You just can't leave it alone, can you? Always interfering, knowing what's best for everyone else. I knew your coming here was going to be a major headache, but it was what Elizabeth wanted. Well, I'll thank you to keep yourself and your opinions out of my way!' Storming from the room, he slammed the outside door behind him.

CHAPTER THREE

A SWIRL of cold winter air chilled Susan's ankles. Guiltily she glanced over at Elizabeth.

'I'm sorry. Burke is right. I was interfering in something that's none of my business.'

Elizabeth shook her head ruefully. 'Burke doesn't take kindly to someone telling him he's wrong. Sometimes I think he's been the boss too long. Just leave him be,' she advised. 'He's so wrapped up in the family business, he has trouble understanding Randy's lack of interest. It bothers him when Randy sleeps in, like this morning. Don't worry. Burke's as stubborn as they come, but he's honest with himself. He only wants what's best for Randy.'

Susan doubted it, but she was reluctant to disagree with Elizabeth, so she was relieved when their conversation was interrupted by the arrival of the dark-haired woman she had seen in the hall the evening before.

'Susan,' said Elizabeth, 'I didn't have an opportunity to introduce you last night. This is Vera Ramirez, the real boss of this house. Without Vera, we'd have fallen apart at the seams long ago. Vera, I'd like you to meet Susan Osborne. Susan is the woman who saved my life.'

The housekeeper slicked back coal-black hair which was already tidily encased in a tight bun, and quickly wiped her hands on her snow-white apron before extending her hand to Susan. 'I'm happy to meet you, Miss Osborne. Everyone here at the ranch is very grateful to you.'

Susan could feel herself blushing. 'Please, call me Susan.' She shook the other woman's hand. 'You mustn't believe Elizabeth's exaggerations. I didn't do that much.'

Elizabeth stubbornly shook her head. 'You certainly did! I don't know what I would have done without you. Whenever I think of that knife——!' She shuddered.

'Don't think of it,' said Vera practically. 'There are more important things to think about today.'

'Vera refuses to allow me to feel sorry for myself,' Elizabeth laughingly complained. 'And, as usual, she's right. I'm expecting Tiffany and Ronnie here some time this afternoon. I thought Burke would go meet them at the airport in Denver, but evidently, Senator Payton made arrangements for his manager to pick them up.'

'Why do you call him Senator Payton?' Susan asked curiously. 'I haven't lived in Denver all that long, but I thought I knew the names of both of the Senators.'

'Ronald was a State Senator years ago. The name just sort of stuck around here. Maybe because he looks so much like a Senator should. He retired from politics years ago when Tiffany's mother died so he could spend more time with his daughter.'

Vera added as she swiftly cleared the dirty dishes from the table, 'It's too bad that the Senator didn't remarry and have more children. It would have been better for Tiffany.'

'You're right, of course,' Elizabeth agreed. 'She's a lovely person, but sometimes I think she could use a little more grit.' She explained further to Susan, 'The Senator and a succession of housekeepers coddled her too much. Speaking of housekeeping, if you wouldn't mind helping me to get Tiffany's room ready, I'd appreciate it. Vera and her girls have already cleaned it, but the beds need sheets, and I thought we might add some nice touches.'

Hours later, Susan stepped back and surveyed the finished room. A basket of bright red poinsettias contrasted gaily with starched white curtains and deep green spreads. With the red and green floral wallpaper, the room might have been designed just for the Christmas holidays. From somewhere, Elizabeth had unearthed a battered teddy bear, which now perched on one of the beds, a perky red bow tied under the bear's lop-sided chin.

'Well, Mr Bear, what do you think? Will the ladies appreciate the basket of red soaps and the books we found for Ronnie to read?' Susan picked up one that she had read to her own kindergarten class only last week. 'I wonder if Ronnie will think this is as funny as my kids did,' she mused out loud.

'Who are you talking to?' Elizabeth walked through the door carrying a stack of freshly laundered towels.

'To Mr Bear, here. He says he's anxious to meet the expected residents of this room, and I have to admit, so am I.'

Elizabeth looked at the glass-domed clock on the fireplace mantel. 'Well, they shouldn't be long now.' The faint sound of door chimes drifted through the bedroom door. Elizabeth laughed. 'That's what I call right on cue.' The two women headed out of the door and down the curved staircase.

A blast of cold air heralded the arrival of a merry group. 'Look who I found on the doorstep,' proclaimed a laughing voice as Randy greeted his mother from behind a precarious load of gaily wrapped packages.

The loud voices must have alerted Burke, and he stepped from his office to merge with the newly-arrived crowd, swiftly embracing the diminutive, fur-clad woman who stood with her back to the stairs. His enthusiastic greeting was in vivid contrast to the chilly reception he had afforded Susan. The uncomfortable feeling of being an outsider at this warm and happy reunion began to steal over Susan. She was just considering the possibility of sneaking back upstairs to her room when Burke spied her standing overhead. The momentary tightening of his lips told Susan her presence had reminded him of their breakfast table conversation. Immediately her chin went up a notch, a gesture of challenge that the glint in his eye acknowledged.

When he spoke, however, his voice was pleasant as he bid her to come down the stairs and meet their company. With his arm still casually draped over the new arrival's shoulders, he turned her to face Susan. Susan gasped. Nothing that Elizabeth had said had prepared her for the woman who faced her. A mass of long black curls tumbled artlessly to frame a face of exotic beauty, with translucent milky white skin and full, pouting lips. Her petite figure was undeniably voluptuous, the curves enhanced by the frills and ruffles of a lavender dress the same shade as her huge eyes. Instantly Susan felt gawky and every bit of her five feet eight inches. Burke's impatient hand gestured her over, and reluctantly she left the sanctuary of the staircase.

'Tiffany, I'd like you to meet Elizabeth's friend, Susan Osborne. Susan, this is Tiffany Tallerton, an old friend of the family.'

'No woman nearing thirty likes to hear herself described as an 'old' friend,' Tiffany protested laughingly to Burke before turning to Susan. 'It's so nice to meet you.' She spoke in a low, breathless voice accompanied by a smile that immediately charmed a responsive one from Susan.

Before Susan could do more than murmur polite greetings, a small whirlwind rushing through the open door engaged everyone's attention, and Susan turned to see a small girl about six or seven years old running towards them, her dark brown pigtails flying behind as she rushed up to Burke and clutched at his leg. 'Hello, Burke!' Her shrill voice was breathless from running.

'Hello, Ronnie.' He grinned down at her.

'How many times have I told you not to run in the house?' asked Tiffany, the resignation in her voice making it plain that this was an oft-spoken and seldom heard complaint. 'What will Burke think of you?'

'He won't care. I'm his girl-friend.' A defiant toss of pigtails punctuated the statement as she swung on Burke's leg.

Tiffany sighed. 'My daughter, Ronnie,' she explained to Susan. 'Ronnie, this is Miss Osborne.'

Solemn blue eyes surveyed Susan from head to foot. Never pausing in her swinging on Burke's leg, the little girl scowled. 'I don't like you.'

Taken aback, Susan could only helplessly ask, 'Why?'

' 'Cos you're a teacher, and I hate teachers.'

'Ronnie!' Appalled, Tiffany turned helplessly in Burke's direction.

He was frowning at the child. 'Veronica, you will apologise to Susan for that rude remark!'

'You know I hate the name Veronica,' the little girl cried. 'Don't call me that!'

Burke raised an warning eyebrow at her. 'Veronica is what I'll call you when I don't like how you behave. Like now, when you were rude to Susan.'

Evidently Burke reserved the right to be rude for himself, Susan thought acidly.

Burke and the girl stared at each other. The child was the first to back down. She turned to Susan. 'Hello, Miss Osborne. I'm sorry I was rude.' She paused, and then, limpid eyes slanting slyly up at Burke, she added, 'Some teachers are mean.'

Susan saw Burke bite his lower lip to prevent a smile before he replied coolly, 'Elizabeth says that Susan is a nice teacher.'

Ronnie gave Susan a doubtful look. 'Are you?'

'I try to be,' answered Susan gravely. 'Besides, right now I'm on vacation. I enjoy vacations just as much as you probably do.'

Ronnie cocked her head. 'I didn't know that teachers liked vacations,' she said slowly, thinking over this novel idea. 'Do you like break time, too?'

'Some days that's my favourite subject,' Susan said with feeling.

'That must be when you play cards,' said Ronnie knowingly.

Susan was baffled. 'Play cards?'

'You know. Play cards,' the thin voice insisted. 'Burke told Mama that you were the Old Maid.'

A stunned silence greeted Ronnie's electrifying statement.

Red starbursts of anger erupted in front of Susan's eyes. She immediately realised that at some time Ronnie had overheard Burke tell Tiffany that Susan was an old maid, and he had not been referring to a childish card game. Before she could explode, however, she caught sight of Ronnie's frightened face. The young girl, sensing the tension in the air, was aware that she had somehow made a grievous mistake. Susan forced a smile. 'I'm really better at Go Fish,' she said. 'Perhaps we can play some time.'

'I don't know how,' said Ronnie hesitantly.

'I'm a teacher, aren't I? I can teach you!'

Her efforts were rewarded by a huge toothy grin of acceptance. Tiffany gave Susan a swift, apologetic smile before quickly shooing her talkative daughter up the staircase in Elizabeth's wake.

Defensively Susan turned to face the ridicule that she was sure Burke and Randy must be sharing. Embarrassment reddening his face, Randy mumbled about the luggage and quickly escaped up the staircase burdened with his packages.

No such embarrassing feelings troubled Burke as he eyed Susan coolly. 'I suppose that you expect some sort of apology from me.'

'Certainly not,' she replied, pleased that her voice hid the hurt engendered by his contemptuous remark to Tiffany. 'I know better than to expect politeness from you.'

Burke laughed, adding, 'Most women would have come unglued at Ronnie's comment. You weren't even fazed. No one would ever doubt that you're a schoolteacher.'

'Don't you mean "Old Maid" schoolteacher?' Susan flashed.

'The remark did sting!' Burke observed in some surprise. 'It shouldn't. You must know that anyone who saw you would see at once how far off the mark I was. Still, it was a stupid remark to make, and for that, I apologise. Ronnie must have heard me talking when I was visiting them last month in New York. I'm sorry she repeated what she overheard.'

'It doesn't matter,' Susan replied coolly, hoping that Burke didn't notice the catch in her voice. She turned away.

Burke caught her arm, a frown darkening his face. 'Yes, it does,' he insisted. 'I pride myself on fighting my battles face to face, but having to listen to Elizabeth constantly praise you is enough to make anyone's blood boil. I could hardly hurt my mother's feelings by pointing out the faults of her "perfect angel". I guess the frustration of having to hide my feelings about you in front of Elizabeth just boiled over when Tiffany asked me if you were as wonderful as Elizabeth painted you.'

'You're jealous,' she accused.

'No way! Just curious as to what you hope to gain from this "friendship" with Elizabeth.'

'Don't judge me by your own standards!' she snapped furiously. 'Didn't it ever occur to you that I might just like your mother?'

'I considered that. But the fact that you've refused all of her invitations in the past put paid to that notion. Which makes it all the more curious that you suddenly decided to honour us with your presence now.'

'I can't win with you, can I? I'm in the wrong if I

don't visit and you're suspicious of me if I do. You ... you ... you're impossible!' she stormed, unable to think of any words adequate to express her feelings.

Burke frowned. 'You should have fiery red hair, to warn everyone about that hair-trigger temper of yours. I think we'd better agree to a moratorium on the fighting so that we don't ruin Elizabeth's holiday.'

'You have the nerve to say that to me! You started it,' she added childishly. 'And your continual nasty behaviour makes me doubt that I could ever agree with you on anything.'

Burke grinned wryly at her. 'I think that the only thing you and I will ever be able to agree on is that we disagree about everything.'

His unexpected grin disarmed Susan, causing her to stammer as she acknowledged the truth of his assessment. Managing a wan smile, she headed up to join Elizabeth and the others. She could feel him watching her climb the stairs, but she refused to turn around. Burke's lightning-swift change of personality had been entirely too disconcerting for her peace of mind.

Fortunately she didn't see him again until dinner. Ronnie had been in and out of Susan's room all afternoon entertaining her with chatter of the small girl's life in New York. Susan had helped Tiffany unpack, and in so doing, had come up with a pretty good understanding of Tiffany's character. The helpless air that clung to the dark-haired woman was based on her inability to make a decision of even the slightest magnitude without seeking assistance from everyone around her. Susan wanted to shake her when Tiffany had asked for the third time her opinion of what Tiffany should wear to dinner. No doubt this defenceless, indecisive air was exactly what Burke found so appealing. They were certainly suited, Susan thought in disgust. A man who wanted to make everyone's decisions, and a woman who couldn't make any. The perfect couple.

Having ascertained from Elizabeth that the family normally changed for dinner, Susan waited until she heard Burke leave his room before she bathed. She had no desire to risk the events of the previous evening. His abrasive behaviour at their every encounter reinforced her belief that he resented the fact that she alone had taken his measure and shown up his feet of clay. The arrogance of him calling her an old maid just because she had told him a few home truths! She'd had her share of proposals, marriage and otherwise, but it was men like Burke who convinced her that marriage was not for her. Men who always had to rule the lives of those around them. It was her opinion that when a man said he loved you, he thought those words gave him the right to run your life. Years of living under the dominating thumbs of her brothers made her very reluctant to risk her hard-won independence. When, and if, she married, her husband would be a gentle and soft-spoken man, as unlike Burke and her brothers as possible.

She smoothed her bright yellow knitted dress down around her hips and finger-combed her hair. At least Burke had had the grace to admit that he had been unfair. She firmly thrust from her mind the tiny burst of pleasure she'd felt at his remark that anyone could see that she wasn't an old maid. Much more profitable to remember his hints that she was interested in more than his mother's friendship. The man was beyond the pale.

Susan's arrival downstairs was the signal for everyone to head for the dining-room. She gazed about her appreciatively. 'I love this room! It's like stepping back in time.' Rich red wallpaper covered the walls above polished wooden wainscoting. At one end of the room sat an enormous marble-topped sideboard with stained glass panels that glowed like jewels. The huge dining-table, set with rich floral porcelain and glittering crystal glassware, matched the sideboard. She looked up. Hanging from a plaster ceiling rosette centred over the table was a brilliant crystal chandelier. 'That light is so beautiful,' she added.

'You sound surprised,' Burke said sarcastically. 'What were you expecting? Tin cups and plates and the trusty hunting knife to pick our teeth?'

Susan flushed with annoyance. So much for Burke's moratorium. He just couldn't resist any chance to needle her. 'I was expecting more utilitarian surroundings,' she snapped. 'Certainly not an exquisite chandelier like that.'

'Be careful,' Randy warned, 'or you'll get coerced into cleaning it. Mom hates the job.'

'I suppose it is a lot of work,' Susan conceded.

Tiffany laughed. 'That chandelier has been a bone of contention in this family for years. Uncle Jim bought it against Elizabeth's wishes while they were on a trip to Ireland.'

'Uncle Jim?'

'My husband, James,' Elizabeth explained. 'I wanted something plain and simple, but James just

went bonkers when he saw that silly thing, and had
to have it. I told him that if he wanted it, he had to
clean it. Of course, he bought it thinking he could get
round me, but I was firm.'

'Stubborn is really the word you want, isn't it?'
Burke asked drily. 'She and Vera formed a conspir-
acy. Dubbing it Gerard's Folly, they absolutely
refused to have anything to do with it. Dad loved
that light and was always polishing it.'

'Why don't you sell it, Elizabeth, if you dislike it so
much?' asked Susan.

'Don't be silly,' Burke said in disgust. 'Elizabeth
would rather get rid of Randy than the chandelier.'
Engaging his mother in private conversation, Burke
made it quite clear that the subject was closed.

Feeling like a small child who had been unjustly
slapped, Susan turned to Randy who was seated
beside her. 'I don't understand,' she said in
bewilderment.

'The truth is, the chandelier was kind of a private
joke between Mom and Dad, a part of the special
something that they shared. Burke explained it to me
once. Dad was a hard-bitten old rancher, and that
light was probably his one frivolous act. The light is
special to Mom because of Dad, but she won't admit
it, sort of in his honour, if you know what I mean.'

'Yes,' Susan said slowly, 'I think I do.' She looked
overhead at the hundreds of crystal prisms catching
the light and sending it spinning about the room. 'I
suppose she really doesn't mind cleaning it now.'

Randy chortled. 'Guess again. Burke cleans it.'

'Burke!'

'Sure. He says he's helping Mom sustain her act.'

The thought of Burke showing such insight and

sensitivity astounded Susan. She never in a million years would have believed him capable of performing what he surely felt was a tedious, female-orientated chore as a gesture of loving consideration towards his mother. She looked down the table where Burke was teasing a laughing Ronnie. The small child appeared to adore him. As a kindergarten teacher, Susan approved of his treatment of the small child. He never talked down to her, but showed genuine interest in her chatter and activities.

Susan blinked her eyes to fend off unexpected tears. She felt like such an outsider in this cosy family group, but now was a foolish time to succumb to self-pity. That was what had got her here in the first place. She should have realised that spending the holidays here was no substitute for her own family. It was different for Tiffany; she had known the Gerards all her life.

She looked across the table to where Tiffany was listening to Burke's and Ronnie's conversation with a slight smile on her face. A clinging dress of shocking pink georgette with a high, ruffled collar gave the illusion of innocence, but the sheer fabric allowed tantalising glimpses of a shadowy vee to show above the low-cut bodice lining. The sweet face of an angel combined with the body of a temptress. Susan sighed. There was no denying that Tiffany's personality was as sweet as her face. No wonder Burke had been devastated by her as a youngster! Whatever his present feelings were, he hid them well behind a mask of warm and courteous friendship, treating Tiffany much as he treated her daughter.

'Susan?' Randy's impatient tone told Susan that he had been speaking to her for some time.

'I'm sorry, I'm afraid I was wool-gathering,' she admitted, embarrassed at her lapse.

Randy laughed. 'Not here, you don't.' He took pity on her confused face and added with a patronising air, 'This is a cattle ranch. We don't gather wool here.'

Susan laughed dutifully at what was obviously an old family joke, and gave him her complete attention.

'I asked if you agreed with Burke about my joining the Peace Corps.'

'I think that's a decision that you and Burke have to make,' Susan answered cautiously. Burke's sardonic nod of approbation exploded her circumspection. 'I certainly believe that Peace Corps volunteers serve useful functions.' Heedless of the growing storm on Burke's face, Susan rushed ahead. 'If you want to volunteer for the Peace Corps, I think you ought to do so no matter what Burke says. After all, it's your life.'

'I told Randy I have no objection to his joining the Peace Corps,' Burke said through clenched teeth. 'If you'd been listening earlier, you would be aware that the topic under discussion is whether it would be worthwhile for him to finish school first. I would have thought that you, as a teacher, would agree with me about the value of a good education no matter what course one pursues in later life.'

Susan's eyes widened. Could Burke possibly be conceding Randy's right to decide his own future? Or was he simply playing for time?

Before she could admit that Burke was right about the schooling, Randy spoke up. 'To tell you the truth, I've been having second thoughts about joining the

Peace Corps. What do you think about law school, Burke?' he asked disarmingly as Susan choked on her wine.

Burke shot Susan a look of triumph before giving Randy a non-committal answer. The glint in his eye warned her that he was not taking lightly what he would view as her latest interference.

Elizabeth pushed her chair away from the table. 'Poor Ronnie is about to fall asleep.' She smiled down at the young girl. 'Let me help you tuck her in, Tiffany.'

Burke immediately stood and helped his mother up from her chair. Susan rose to follow the others from the room, but Burke's broad body blocked her exit. Slamming shut the door, he relentlessly backed her up against the wall, a hand on either side of her. She was aware of his muscled arms and great strength as he lightly pressed against her. His chest brushed hers, a searing touch, and she forced herself to look steadily into his face. Dark grey eyes glared fiercely down at her.

'Let me go!' Was that breathless voice hers?

'Not until we reach an understanding. I want you to stop interfering in things you know nothing about.'

'Don't you mean you want me to stop challenging your authority over the rest of the world?' she taunted.

An odd, brooding look passed over Burke's face. 'You do insist on challenging me. I wonder why.'

'You know why. I just don't happen to think that you're an all-seeing god who knows what's best for everyone else.'

'Is that really why you challenge me? I think it's

something much more basic than that. I'm probably the first man you've met that you haven't been able to bring to his knees. You're a lady who's just looking for a man to master her.'

'That's exactly the chauvinistic garbage I'd expect from you! Do you really think I'd be interested in a big bad cowboy who thinks he can throw his weight around?'

'Let's find out, shall we?'

'No!' she gasped, guessing his intent. One large hand encircled her neck while his head descended with lightning speed. Expecting harshness, she was disarmed by lips, soft and gentle, that caressed hers with light, soothing kisses. In spite of her willing it otherwise, she could feel her body responding to Burke's expertise. That was all it was. She couldn't be attracted to a man who wanted nothing more than to physically dominate her. With her last ounce of willpower she pushed at him. He stepped back, but she didn't kid herself that her strength was any match for his.

'What is it about you that drives me up the wall? I don't usually lose my temper with women,' said Burke, shaking his head ruefully. 'I always tell myself that I will very calmly discuss my point of view with you, and the next thing I know we're in a slanging match.'

'You know very well why you dislike me,' Susan explained furiously. 'I'm the only person around who doesn't worship at your feet!'

'Then it appears that our dislike is mutual,' Burke replied coolly. Without a backward glance, he exited from the dining-room.

Leaving behind a limp and drained Susan. Now

that Burke's hard body was no longer pressing her
against the wall, her legs threatened to collapse
beneath her, and she clutched at a nearby chair.
Burke was every bit the bully, the tyrant, the
arrogant, self-centred beast that she had expected.
He had stood right here and told her to keep her
mouth shut when he was bossing everyone around.
There had been nothing romantic intended in his
kiss. If he couldn't intimidate her, then he would try
another way of controlling her. She'd show him.
With shaky fingers she traced the outline of her lips.
Was it her imagination that she could still feel
Burke's lips on hers?

Several hours later she prepared for bed, thankful
that no matter how swollen and throbbing her lips
felt, at least no one else appeared to notice anything
wrong. Not that they had much opportunity to do so.
Tiffany, having safely tucked Ronnie away for the
evening, had borrowed one of the ranch cars to drive
over to her father's place. Randy was meeting
friends in town, and Burke had retired to his office.
That left Elizabeth and Susan watching a Christmas
special on television. At least, Susan assumed that
Elizabeth had watched it. When Elizabeth clicked
off the set and enthused about the programme, Susan
discovered, to her annoyance, that she had no idea
what it had been about. Luckily, Elizabeth had been
so affected by the story's plot that she failed to realise
that Susan was contributing little to their conversation. Shortly after that, Elizabeth had announced her
intention of retiring for the night, and Susan had
gone up with her, thankful to escape to the solitude
of her bedroom where she could analyse her
ambivalent feelings about Burke's kiss.

As it turned out, however, solitude was not to be hers. Answering her door in response to a light knock, Susan discovered Tiffany in the doorway.

'I'm too keyed up to go to bed,' the other woman announced. 'Mind if I come in?'

Susan stepped back in wordless invitation, and Tiffany glided past, trailed by the spicy scent of her perfume. Her cheeks were still rosy from the night air, evidence that she had just returned. 'I thought we could talk and get to know each other better. I've heard so much about you from Elizabeth. How nice for her that you could come for the holidays; don't your own relatives object?'

'I'm afraid there are only my two brothers. Tom is a Commander in the Navy, and he's been stationed in Japan since June. And, Mike, my other brother, is in the Air Force in Germany.'

'That's hard on you,' said Tiffany sympathetically. 'But I have to envy you having brothers. I always hated being an only child. I would have liked having older brothers around to give me guidance.'

'Guidance! Orders are more like it! My brothers tried to run my entire life for me; I had to fight them every step of the way in every decision that I ever made.' Susan spoke with feeling. Although she adored her two brothers, normally the more distance between them, the better. Their parents having died when the trio were quite young, the three had spent their formative years being shunted from relative to relative. Her brothers, eight and ten years older than Susan, had from the beginning assumed a protective stance toward their younger sister. At first appreciative, Susan soon rebelled against such cosseting care. Life was often a war zone, with her brothers assuring her that they knew what was best for her, and Susan asserting that she could make her own decisions.

'But surely they loved you and had your best interests at heart?' Tiffany protested.

'Of course they did,' answered Susan. That fact only made her feel guilty; it never caused her to give up her struggles. Boy-friends, college problems, career goals—all had run the gauntlet of the two males who considered themselves self-appointed arbiters of her life.

'Are your brothers married?'

'Yes, both of them, and Tom has two adorable little boys.' When they had each, in turn, married, she had hoped that their concerns would be for their wives instead of her. On the contrary. They seemed to have infected their wives with the same belief that Susan was totally incapable of leading her life without their interference.

'How did you happen to end up out here in Colorado?' asked Tiffany curiously.

'Well, it's rather a long story. My brothers decided I should stay with an aunt who was living in a small town in Nebraska and teach there. Naturally I couldn't let them decide my life, so I moved to Omaha. Then Mike said that he was being transferred to Offutt Air Force Base, which is near there, so I immediately applied for a job in Aurora.'

'But I thought you said your brother was in Germany.'

'That's the crazy part,' she admitted. 'After I'd made all my arrangements to move to Denver, Mike discovered that he was being sent to Europe. Once again I'd reacted instead of acted,' she said drily. Regretting her usual impulsive behaviour, she had reluctantly moved to Denver, giving up friends and starting her life all over again. However, once in the Mile-High city, Susan had rapidly come under Denver's spell and regarded her hasty decision as an extremely lucky one.

Until now. Almost two weeks of vacation to get through before she could escape back to her apartment. Maybe it wouldn't be so bad, she told herself hopefully. Elizabeth was pleased at her visit, Randy and Tiffany were certainly congenial, and Ronnie was unquestionably a sweet child. All she had to do was keep out of Burke's way.

Tiffany returned to her earlier thought. 'Maybe you did have to fight to get your own way,' she said. 'But don't you see? That put steel in your backbone.' Tiffany gave a bitter little laugh. 'My backbone is pure marshmallow.'

'I'm sure that's not true,' Susan demurred.

'Yes, it is,' insisted Tiffany. 'With my mother dying when I was so young, I'm afraid Daddy wrapped me in cotton wool. He couldn't face anything happening to me.' She added thoughtfully, 'I really envy you.'

'You envy me?' Susan repeated, dumbfounded.

'You're so independent. You don't need a man to lean on. I went straight from my father's care to my husband's. At an age when most girls are off to college trying out their wings, I was here keeping house for Dad, planning my wedding to Burke.' Tiffany smiled shyly at Susan. 'I'm sure you've heard that I was engaged to Burke before I ran off and married Steve.'

'Well, yes, I'd heard something about it,' she admitted.

'It doesn't show me in a good light, I realise. Daddy wanted me to marry Burke, and I was agreeable until Steve came along. I fell head over heels in love with him, and he insisted we get married. I knew that Daddy wouldn't like it. Running away just seemed easier than listening to all the shouting.'

'Surely your father wanted you to be happy?' suggested Susan delicately.

Tiffany shrugged. 'Of course he did. The problem was, Daddy seldom consulted me on what would make me happy.' She paused, before adding reflectively, 'Daddy, Burke, Steve—they all told me what to do, and it always seemed easier to do what they wanted than to argue.' At Susan's look of disgust, she added defensively, 'They meant well. They wanted what was best for me.'

'But Tiffany, how could they know what's best for you? Surely you are the only person qualified to know that.'

'I know. It sounds so reasonable when you say it.' Her voice trailed off. 'Men get so loud when you disagree with them. I don't like shouting and arguing. Life was always so much more pleasant when I agreed with them.' She laughed ruefully. 'I sound like a real weakling, don't I? Letting Daddy push me to marry Burke, and Steve push me to elope. Burke was the only one who seemed to understand when I explained.'

'He didn't argue with you?' Susan asked curiously.

'He wanted me to be happy,' replied Tiffany simply. 'He even volunteered to give the news to Daddy.'

Susan choked. 'You told Burke but not your father?'

'I had to give Burke back his ring before I married Steve, didn't I? To do otherwise wouldn't have been fair to Burke. He knew that Daddy would talk me out of marrying Steve if I saw him before the wedding. He drove us straight to the airport, and then came back and told Daddy, so Daddy wouldn't worry when I didn't come home that night. Steve wouldn't let me call Daddy until the next day—until we were good and married, he said.'

'How kind of Burke,' said Susan weakly. It seemed strange to her that Burke had allowed Steve to practically bully Tiffany into marriage. He must have been so hurt by Tiffany's telling him that she was in love with someone else that he had let her go without a struggle. Tiffany's explanation that Burke wanted her to be happy was hard to credit. 'Were you happy?' she asked.

'Oh yes, marvellously so. Steve was wonderful, and so good to me.' Tiffany's voice broke, and she quickly wiped a tear from her cheek. 'When he died, I wanted to die, too. If I hadn't had Ronnie, I don't know what I would have done. And Burke. Burke was a tremendous support to me; Daddy wanted me to come home. I know he saw Steve's death as a second chance for him to get the son-in-law he wanted. Don't get me wrong; Daddy liked Steve. It's just—well, he'd counted on me marrying Burke for years. When I refused to move back here it was Burke who was on my side. He convinced Daddy to leave me alone, and let time heal the wounds.' She grimaced. 'It seems I'm always leaning on Burke.

That's probably why he admires you so much. You're so strong.'

Susan could only stare at Tiffany's startling comment. 'What on earth are you talking about? Burke makes no bones about the fact that he dislikes me.'

'No, no.' Tiffany vigorously shook her black curls. 'He admires the way you rushed to Elizabeth's rescue, and he's grateful for your care of her.'

Susan remained sceptical. 'So grateful he yelled at me and called me all sorts of names?'

'Did he really do that?' Tiffany asked in amazement. At Susan's nod of confirmation, she frowned thoughtfully. 'It's not like Burke not to show his appreciation. You know,' she added slowly, 'Burke has told me several times how he feels he's to blame for Elizabeth's accident.'

'How in the world could it be his fault?'

'Evidently Elizabeth had asked him to drive her up to Denver that day, and he'd said that he was too busy. So then, when she was attacked, of course, Burke felt terribly guilty.'

'I find it hard to believe that Elizabeth would blame Burke for her accident.'

'I'm sure that she doesn't,' agreed Tiffany. 'What you have to understand is how Burke thinks. He's been the man of the house and in charge of other people's lives for so long that he's come to think of himself as a little god-like. He takes care of so many of us, doing what he feels is best, and usually, he's right. Everyone is always thanking him and saying how wonderful he is. Sometimes I think he's become a little smug about it all. So when it appeared that he failed to take proper care of his mother—well . . . Let

me finish,' she forestalled Susan's interruption. 'He's
embarrassed and angry at himself because he thinks
he let Elizabeth down, and of course, that anger
carries over a little to you, because after all, you're
the one who was forced to be a substitute for him.'

'You mean he resents the fact that I took better
care of his mother than he did,' said Susan drily.

Tiffany shook her head slowly. 'I'm not sure I
would put it quite that way. Burke can hardly be held
accountable for the weather. Daddy said that even
with all his hired hands working around the clock, he
lost some of his new calves. I'm sure it was no
different for Burke. Plus, there were the others to
think about.'

'Others?'

'The smaller ranchers in the area can't afford the
huge calving sheds and heavy equipment that Burke
has, so they're even more vulnerable when bad
weather strikes. Burke organised a massive airdrop
to get feed out to their stranded livestock.'

Susan was startled. 'Burke did that?'

Tiffany elaborated on the blizzard clean-up
operations for some minutes, before she departed,
unsuccessfully trying to hide huge yawns.

She left behind a restive Susan. Burke could have
explained the situation a little more clearly, she
thought resentfully. If she had known how badly he
was needed, then she wouldn't have been so insistent
that he drop everything and visit his mother. *When
did you give him the opportunity to explain further?*
a tiny voice asked her.

She humped her shoulders against her own inner
accusations. Burke should have realised that she
didn't understand. After all, she was a newcomer to

Colorado, and certainly knew nothing about ranch life. Not to mention how upset she was about Elizabeth's mugging and subsequent operation. Anyone would have reacted negatively under so much stress. Where did Burke get off, expecting her to bow instantly to his orders?

Tiffany could defend Burke all she wanted, but that didn't change the fact that he'd been rude, inconsiderate and totally bad-tempered. Maybe he was upset about his mother and bedevilled by a killer storm at the same time. Was that any reason to take out his frustrations on a perfect stranger who was only trying to help? Perhaps her own behaviour was less than impeccable, in the light of Tiffany's disclosures, but she certainly owed no apologies to Burke Gerard. He'd never even thanked her for coming to his mother's assistance.

Besides, if she apologised now, he was just arrogant enough to think that her change of attitude was caused by his kisses. Splashing lotion on her hot cheeks, she tried to put out of her mind the memory of his warm lips on hers. Hoping to divert her thoughts, she slipped between cool sheets and resolutely opened the novel she'd brought with her. The hero of the book was a hard-boiled private detective. He reminded her of Burke.

CHAPTER FOUR

SUSAN awakened suddenly, her heart pounding wildly in the quiet bedroom. Whatever had frightened her was banished with her wakening, but a residue of an unknown fear held her trapped in its grip. Blinking to focus her vision, she gazed anxiously about the room. A half-light from outside bathed the room in a soft glow, enabling her to pick out the dark shapes of the massive old furniture. There was nothing to have caused this unreasonable fear. She must have been having a bad nightmare. Breathing deeply, she sought to slow her racing pulse. Impossible to recall the dream, yet at the same time, she was unable to throw off the paralysing fear it had induced. The light in the room made her wonder if dawn was on its way. She craned her neck to read the illuminated clock on her bedside table. The hands showed it was a few minutes past midnight; the light must be from the moon. She pulled the bedcovers up to her chin and closed her eyes, hoping sleep would not prove elusive.

A hideous howl caused her to bolt upright in fright, the sheet clutched to her chest. The eerie, keening sound was repeated, and she dived under the blankets, cowering there, her hands pressed tightly against her ears in a futile attempt to blot out the spine-chilling cry. Fear rose in choking waves in her throat. Another fiendish yell sent her leaping from her bed, intent on seeking sanctuary. Burke

in his neck. Even the sweet, musky scent of his skin failed to comfort her as the cry seemed to go on for ever. When it finally ceased, she whispered, 'I heard it earlier in my room, and I was so frightened I came in here.'

For a short moment, Burke was rigid, saying nothing, and then he pried Susan's hands from behind his neck. 'Go to the window and don't turn around.'

'Why?' she asked fearfully.

'In the first place so I can get some trousers on, and in the second place so you can see your troublesome noise-maker.'

'Oh.'

'Oh,' he mimicked. 'Unless you'd rather stay here?' he asked provocatively.

'No.' Breathlessly she bolted for the window, Burke's low, amused laugh following her from the bed.

A full moon shone brightly overhead, spotlighting this corner of the ranch yard. The wind blew softly through the encircling tall pines, casting moving shadows on the pale snow. There was a ghostly beauty to the night, and Susan shivered in response.

'Cold?' Burke asked over her shoulder.

The air was chilly by the window, and the wooden floors felt freezing to Susan's bare feet. 'A little,' she admitted.

'Don't you ever dress for the weather?' he grumbled, and she felt him walk away. Seconds later he returned, slipping huge, but warm slippers on her feet. Pulling her to him, he wrapped a quilt tightly around the two of them, encasing them in a cocoon of warmth. Burke's bare chest seemed to burn her through the thin flannel of her gown, and once again she shivered, this time not from cold. She hoped that Burke wouldn't notice. She hoped in vain.

'Still frightened?' he asked. 'Not of me, I hope. I'm not the big bad wolf, you know.' He spoke quietly, his breath disturbing the tendrils of hair about her ear. 'Of course,' he went on, 'if I were, you'd be the one I'd eat first.'

'Why?' In her surprise, the question simply popped out.

'As I remember my fairy tales, the wolf ate Grandmother first. With that nightgown on, all you'd need is a lacy cap to pass for Grandmother,' he teased.

Susan was glad the darkness hid the warm crimson tide that engulfed her face. The old nightgown she was wearing was a relic from college days, that had seen better times. Warmth was its only virtue.

'I should have realised that you didn't plan a midnight assignation when I saw what you were wearing!'

'I'm sure you have more experience than I do in the proper apparel for those matters,' Susan said tartly.

'I'm sure I do.'

Susan's indignant gasp could have been caused by Burke's words or the sudden tightening of his arms. 'There. Over by the trees, at the edge of the clearing. See him?'

A large dog trotted out from the shadows and sat on his haunches, the moon shining directly on him. Lifting his muzzle to the sky, he began to howl, an eerie, mournful sound that chilled Susan. She was glad of Burke's protective clasp, but bewildered at what she saw and heard.

'But ... but ... that's just a German Shepherd dog,' she said at last.

He laughed. 'What a city girl you are! That's a coyote.'

'A coyote!' Susan was thrilled at her first glimpse of the Old West's most resourceful rogue.

The animal gave voice once more, and the couple inside stood quietly listening. From a far hillside a mournful answer floated back. For some minutes the strange communications continued, and then, as if at a signal, the coyote stopped, rose to all four legs and trotted silently back into the shadow of the trees.

Susan leaned back against Burke, releasing her pent-up breath in a long sigh. 'Thank you,' she said shakily. 'That was terrific!'

'You're welcome. The old boy puts on quite a show, doesn't he?'

She nodded.

'You're not frightened any more?'

She shook her head.

'Okay, back to bed with you,' he ordered briskly as he opened the quilt that encased them. The cold draught chilled her, and she took a sudden step, tripping over the hem of her nightgown.

Burke swiftly wrapped the quilt around her again and swept her up in his arms.

'What ... what ... are you doing?' she stammered.

'What big eyes you have, Grandmother,' he taunted. He started towards her room. 'I'm putting you to bed where all good little girls belong.' He unceremoniously dumped her, quilt and all, on her bed and stared down at her, hands on hips. 'Unless, of course, you'd rather be a bad little girl?' he asked, looming above her.

Hoping the dark successfully hid her warm flush, she said, 'No, thank you.'

Burke laughed as he walked to the connecting door.

'Burke?' Susan forced herself to speak. 'I'm sorry,' she faltered, ashamed that she had let her fears run away with her.

'Sorry about what?' he asked coolly. 'Sorry you woke me, or sorry that you exposed a chink in that armour of independence you wear?'

Susan stiffened. 'I'm sorry I bothered you. It won't happen again.'

'I wish I could believe that,' he returned enigmatically. Closing the door firmly behind him, he left.

Susan eyed the closed door with smouldering emotions. He was impossible! From her very first contact with him, she had known that he was the type of man that she disliked the most. Bossy, arrogant, self-centred. And confusing, she thought suddenly. She would have expected ridicule or at least to be patronised for her fears, but Burke had been almost kind. Still wrapped in his quilt, she snuggled deep in its enfolding warmth. Memories of his strong protective arms came back to her as she drifted off to sleep, breathing the heady, masculine scent that clung to his quilt.

The sun was warming her room with its golden beams when Susan next awakened. As she stretched her arms above her head, the sight of Burke's quilt on top of the rippling blankets brought back in a rush the memories of the previous night. Burke had shown her a new and different side to his personality.

Was it possible that the resemblances between him and her brothers had blinded her to the differences?

She felt a warm flush crawl over her body at the recollection that whatever else Burke was, last night he had not treated her in a brotherly fashion. She caught herself up before she could dwell on Burke's kisses. It wasn't so surprising that a man who had wakened from a sound sleep to find a woman in his bed would react in a physical way. She mustn't make the mistake of reading something into his actions that wasn't there. She blushed to think of her own initial response. What must Burke think?

Glancing at the clock, she was relieved to see how late it was. Burke would long ago have headed outside or shut himself up in his office. It would be at least lunchtime before she would have to face him.

Her relief was short-lived. The first person she saw as she walked into the kitchen was Burke, leaning back in his chair, drinking coffee and listening to Ronnie. He looked up as she entered, the gleam of amusement in his eyes quickly suppressed. Refusing to give him the pleasure of knowing how disconcerted she was, she greeted him coolly before speaking to the other three seated at the table. Having learned that Elizabeth kept breakfast warm on the back of the stove, she dished herself up some before joining the others. Eating hungrily, she was content to let the others do the talking.

It was Randy who precipitated the embarrassing moment. 'Anybody else hear Moonlight last night?' he asked around the table.

Curiously Susan looked up to see both Burke and Elizabeth nod their heads.

Ronnie giggled. 'Randy, you're silly. You can't

hear the moon. You can only see it.'

Randy shot the child a superior look. 'I didn't say the moon, Ronnie. I said Moonlight,' he corrected.

Susan knew she must echo Ronnie's look of bewilderment. 'I agree with Ronnie. You can't hear moonlight either.'

'Shows what you know,' Randy retorted. 'Teachers aren't always as smart as they think they are.'

Susan realised that she was being teased, and she looked helplessly at Elizabeth for an explanation, but it was Burke who spoke up.

'You not only heard Moonlight last night, you saw him.'

Susan frowned in puzzlement, but then comprehension quickly dawned. 'Oh,' she said delightedly, 'the coyote! You call the coyote Moonlight.'

Randy laughed. 'Give the teacher an "A". That old guy has been visiting us on moonlit nights for three or four years now. At least,' he qualified, 'we think it's the same one. He sings quite a song, doesn't he?'

'He certainly does. I really enjoyed the show.' Catching the disbelieving lift of Burke's brow, she hastily added, 'I was a little scared at first, but once I saw him and realised that the noise came from a coyote, it was exciting.'

'We're just pulling out all the stops to entertain you,' Randy said. 'You were lucky. Normally you can't see him from the room you're in.'

'Oh, but I wasn't in—that is to say . . .' She looked in confusion at Burke.

With only a slightly mocking look at her predicament, he came to her rescue. 'The noise awakened Susan, and, being a city girl, she was naturally a little

frightened and wanted to know what was going on,
so she woke me up. I knew once she saw her
midnight monster she'd feel more comfortable, so I
invited her to view Moonlight out of my window.'

With Burke's prosaic explanation, the talk around
the table turned to other matters. Susan was relieved
that Burke didn't mention that she had practically
leapt into bed with him out of fear. Suddenly the
omission made her very nervous. She would have
thought that he would have jumped at the chance to
expose any weakness of hers. She eyed him
thoughtfully beneath lowered lashes. To her chagrin,
he was studying her openly. Aware that he had her
attention, his eyes swept her body in a bold, insolent
fashion, with undertones so sensuous that Susan
could almost feel the heat. Burke might not tell her
story in public, but he had no intention of allowing
her to forget her momentary lapse. A flush betrayed
her embarrassment as she remembered his warm,
sinewy body and her own unexpected response to
him.

He chuckled.

'What's so funny about cattle rustling?' demanded
Randy, referring to his present topic of conversation.

'Sorry, my mind must have drifted off,' Burke
answered.

Satisfied, Randy turned to answer a query of his
mother's. Burke held Susan's eyes across the width of
the table. 'I had a different type of conflict in mind.'
He spoke so quietly that Susan wasn't sure if she
actually heard the words or only sensed them.

She refused to allow him to unsettle her further.
'What type of conflict is that?' she questioned in a
low voice, not eager to gain the others' attention.

'The eternal war between men and women,' he replied promptly. No snappy comeback came to Susan's rescue. 'And to the victor goes the spoils,' he added in a soft drawl. He flicked a look at Susan's heaving breast before joining in the general conversation around the breakfast table.

Shaken by the open challenge, Susan clutched spasmodically at the napkin lying in her lap. It wasn't out of consideration for her feelings that Burke had told an edited version of what happened last night. He simply was saving the episode as ammunition for the next time she flaunted his authority. The sexual innuendoes were nothing more than warnings. A typical male chauvinist, he could only deal with her on a sexual level. And because she refused to view him through the same rose-coloured glasses as everyone else did, he resented her very presence in this house. Every time he saw her, he must be reminded how very much she held him in contempt. By putting her down, he hoped to restore his own tarnished image. Well, just let him try. He'd soon find that he'd met his match in Susan Osborne. All her life she had been fighting the notion of male superiority, and having held her own with two brothers, she wasn't about to be defeated by six feet plus of lazy, sexual masculinity.

Fortunately for the sake of Susan's nerves, Burke and Randy were just passing through, having breakfasted hours earlier, and they were soon on their way back to work. After breakfast, Susan wandered into Elizabeth's sitting-room where Elizabeth was reading a book out loud to Ronnie.

Like Elizabeth herself, her sitting-room was soft and plush, with flowers everywhere—in the carpet, on the walls, covering the chairs and sofas, down the curtains, in prints and in paintings. The effect was of sitting in a flower garden. Books on wildlife were piled in comfortable profusion around the room, while bird figurines, flowered bowls and Oriental vases decorated table tops. Any remaining space was taken up by photographs, Elizabeth as a bride and young mother, her husband—a tall, broad man who resembled Burke—and numerous photographs of Elizabeth's sons from infancy to manhood.

It was the photographs that drew Susan's attention. In spite of her will not to, again and again she was compelled to study all the different pictures of Burke. She was especially attracted to a study of the three-year-old boy who sat tall and proud on his first pony, disdaining to clutch the saddle horn. The photo of a triumphant younger Burke, robed in cap and gown and holding aloft his college diploma, always made her wonder how Tiffany could have rejected the laughing, vibrant young man who exhibited such zest and promise. Tiffany had said she had been happy with her husband, but Susan wondered how often the other woman had sat in this room, and seeing that picture, regretted her elopement. If she had, she must be doubly grateful to be getting a second chance.

In a more recent picture, the photographer had caught Burke at work. Mud-spattered jeans, a stetson pulled low over his forehead, and a sweat-stained shirt could not detract from the sexual magnetism Burke exuded. Rolled-up sleeves exposed his hard, sinewy arms, reminding Susan of how those same arms had felt so warm and comforting wrapped around her. The image of him asleep with his shoulders and back bared as he had been the previous night, teased at her mind. Try as she might to forget, she could almost feel his silken skin and hard muscles beneath her hands. She shook her head to rid herself of such disquieting thoughts.

She was reacting to Burke's physical presence like a teenager with overactive glands. Was her life so unsatisfactory that she was starting to fantasise? She thought about Tiffany. Not that much older than Susan, the other woman had already jilted one lover, married, had a child and been widowed. At twenty-four, Susan couldn't even claim the lover. She had dated any number of men, but not one had stirred her blood enough to allow him into her bedroom. The truth was that she had always been afraid that if she did give herself to a man, he would demand total ownership of her life as well as her body. She wasn't ready to take that chance. Now she wondered if she'd been reading too much into the act of sex. Perhaps if she had taken a more casual approach years ago, Burke's blatant sexuality wouldn't affect her so. Maybe her problem *was* in her glands. Magazines always made it sound so simple, this tricky sexual business between male and female. What she probably needed was a good rousing love affair, and then those tight jeans that Burke strolled around in would be nothing more than blue denim.

'A day like today certainly forecasts that Christmas is only a couple of days away.' Elizabeth's voice interrupted Susan's thoughts.

Susan looked out of the window. A fresh wet snow had fallen while she slept, and all the trees and shrubs were coated in a thin sheath of white, creating a fairy wonderland. The warm morning sun, which danced off the snow and dazzled the eyes, was melting the snow on the trees, sending it crashing to the ground in powdery white explosions. She agreed with Elizabeth before asking, 'When do you put up your Christmas tree?'

Elizabeth gazed with consternation at her. 'I forgot all about a tree! I hate to say this, but it's been several years since we've put one up,' she admitted. 'But with Ronnie here, of course we have to put up a tree.'

'I love Christmas trees,' Ronnie confided.

'Me, too.' Elizabeth hugged the small girl beside her. 'I've missed celebrating the holidays with all the traditions we used to keep. After the boys were grown, they lost interest, and it wasn't much fun decorating a tree all by myself, but if you girls won't mind helping me, I'd love to have a tree again. After all, what's Christmas without a tree?'

The decision made, Elizabeth was anxious to get started. 'Why don't you go run get your coat, Ronnie, and get permission from your mom. Maybe she'd like to go along.'

Ronnie readily agreed and left the room. Elizabeth stood up, frowning down on Susan. 'I hope you have some warmer clothes than those you were wearing the night you arrived.' At Susan's nod, she added, 'I'll lend you some boots if you need them. Hard telling how much the snow may have drifted in places.'

Elizabeth's remarks made little sense to Susan. 'One would think that the roads to town would be all cleared by now.'

'To town?' Elizabeth snorted. 'We're not going to town.'

'I thought we were going to get a tree.'

'We are,' Elizabeth explained patiently. 'With all this land, we certainly ought to be able to find ourselves a suitable tree. We'll just go and chop one down.'

'Chop one down? Won't Burke be angry about that?'

'Don't be silly; Burke won't care.'

'Burke won't care about what?' asked Burke as he entered the room behind Tiffany. 'Seems to me those words could get you in a heap of trouble, Elizabeth.'

'Don't be ridiculous! We've decided that we need a Christmas tree, and I said we could find a tree somewhere on the ranch to use.'

'You decided?' Burke drawled. 'Or Susan decided?'

'Susan brought it up, but I should have thought of it sooner.'

Burke frowned. 'I'm not sure that a tree is a good idea.'

Irritated by his negative remarks, Susan couldn't hold her tongue. 'Don't tell me you're a Scrooge, too,' she snapped.

He raised his eyebrows at her tone. 'I simply thought that a tree might be too much work for Elizabeth.'

'Nonsense,' said his mother briskly. 'Susan and Ronnie have promised to do all the work. I'm just going to supervise.'

How like Burke to put her in the wrong, Susan thought furiously. Trying to make it appear that she was selfishly demanding a tree at the expense of Elizabeth's health. She glared at his back as he turned to his mother with instructions.

'There's a good-looking stand of trees down in the south pasture where the creek makes a sharp right turn. I think you'll find a satisfactory tree there.'

Thirty minutes later, when Susan joined the others, bundled up as they were against the winter chill, she discovered that Randy had been tapped by Burke to accompany the women on their tree-cutting expedition. Elizabeth and Ronnie were both cosily ensconced in the back seat of the ranch pick-up, with Ronnie bouncing up and down in her eagerness. Obeying the small girl's exhortations to hurry, Susan quickly slid into the front seat beside Randy. Burke's hand, firmly anchored on the door, prevented her from closing it as he leaned across her to speak to Randy. Trying to ignore the scent of soap and leather that clung to him, she concentrated instead on the way his blond hair curled above his jacket. Fingers that itched to play with the tendrils were firmly jammed into her pockets.

Finishing his conversation with Randy, he slowly brushed once more past Susan. This time, however, he murmured in her ear in passing, 'I may be Scrooge, but you do a great imitation of Katharina.' Shutting the door on her uncomprehending look, he waved them off with a big sweep of his hat. For the next fifteen minutes, Susan ignored the swirl of conversation around her as she puzzled out who Katharina was. The answer, when it came to her, prompted a gasp of indignation. He'd called her a shrew!

'Sorry about that,' Randy smiled over at her in apology.

Susan stared at him blankly, until another patch of icy snow had them slithering in the direction of the ditch and her grabbing the door handle. As Randy confidently brought the truck back under control, she realised that he had misunderstood the cause of her gasp.

'Where's your mother?' she called over her shoulder to Ronnie.

'Burke was going over to Grandpa Payton's ranch, and she decided to go with him.'

Lucky for them they had her around to babysit while they did their romancing, Susan thought in annoyance, totally ignoring the fact that Elizabeth and Randy were present. But her disgruntled attitude was no match for Ronnie's contagious spirits which pervaded the whole cab; even Susan had to smile as the child commanded Randy to drive faster, a command that Randy, thank goodness, disregarded. Instead he started Ronnie singing silly Christmas songs, and soon the air rang with questionable music and giggles as they all joined in. Randy's bringing the truck to a halt was the signal to stop the singing. 'We're here,' he announced unnecessarily. A stand of evergreens in all shapes and sizes dominated the brush-covered land.

'Burke was right. There are some nice trees here,' said Elizabeth, a pleased look on her face.

Susan jumped out of the truck, the spicy pine scent tickling her nostrils. 'They're all so lovely. It seems a shame to cut one of these down.' As the others walked through the stand of trees, exclaiming over first one, and then another, she went on her own treasure hunt. Finding what she sought, she called the others to her side. 'How about that tree?' she suggested.

'Where?' Randy asked in bewilderment, doubting

the direction of her pointing finger.

'Right here,' Susan answered, continuing to point to a misshapen tree a few yards from them. 'That tree is perfect.'

Ronnie giggled from behind Randy. 'Susan, that tree is silly-looking! It bends over and wiggles and has only one side. Look, there aren't any branches at the back.'

'Exactly,' said Susan decisively. 'Mother Nature made the other trees beautiful, but it's up to us to do something for this poor guy. Pretty decorations will give him a new lease on life, and besides, cutting this one down won't bother anyone.'

Elizabeth and Randy eyed the scraggy tree doubtfully. 'I think we can find a better one,' said Elizabeth hesitantly. 'Wouldn't you prefer a more cylindrical tree?'

'I hate to cut down a beautiful one. It seems such a waste. What do you think, Ronnie?' she appealed.

Ronnie giggled. 'Burke will kill us if we bring that tree home,' she said, sounding remarkably adult.

Sensing Susan's determination, Randy walked around the tree. 'Maybe it won't be too bad. We can set it in the corner, and just decorate the front side. If I cut off a few branches here and wire them there,' he poked among the evergreen boughs.

'That's a great idea, Randy. Thank you.' Susan turned to the others. 'Well, what do you think?'

Elizabeth shrugged. 'It's up to the rest of you. If this is the tree you want, go ahead.'

'Elizabeth,' Ronnie piped up, 'remember the story you read me about the tree that felt so bad because everyone said he was so ugly and no one wanted him for a Christmas tree?' At the older woman's nod, the small girl continued, 'Well, we don't want this tree to feel bad, do we?'

'All right, this tree it is,' Randy laughed. 'Just remember when Burke blows a gasket, this wasn't my idea.'

'If you really think he'll be angry . . .?' Susan turned to Elizabeth in concern.

'Nonsense. Randy is just teasing. Burke couldn't care less if we even have a tree. He'll never even notice that this one is—er—a little different.'

'You just wait until we finish with it. It will be . . . the most beautiful tree you've ever seen,' Susan guaranteed rashly.

'It will! It will!' Ronnie dashed up to the tree and hugged the trunk. 'You'll be the happiest tree in Colorado,' she promised.

Randy pulled a chain saw from the back of the truck and soon the loud, whirring sound of sawing filled the air. Elizabeth and Ronnie wandered down to the stream and poked at the ice with a long stick, and Susan strolled through the trees enjoying the fresh scent of the pines and the scolding of squirrels, indignant that their territory had been invaded.

Randy finished sawing down the tree in no time at all, and the twisted pine was installed in the back of the pick-up for the return ride to the ranch house.

An hour later Randy stepped back and surveyed the evergreen tree that sprawled in the corner. 'There, that's not so bad, is it?' he asked optimistically.

Ronnie laughed. 'It looks funny with no back and all those branches tied on in front.'

'It's just right,' Susan interjected hastily. 'You did a lovely job of shaping the tree, and after we put on the ornaments, it will look fabulous.'

Randy gave her a quizzical took before turning to his mother. 'What do you think, Mom?'

Elizabeth cocked her grey head to one side and carefully surveyed the tree. 'I think Susan has more imagination than I have,' she at last admitted.

Susan was stricken with doubts. After all, this was the older woman's home. 'If you really don't like this tree, we could go and select another.'

'After all my work?' asked Randy indignantly.

'I love this tree,' Ronnie added defiantly.

Elizabeth laughed. 'We wouldn't dare, would we? Besides, I applaud the sentiment behind your selection. I'm sure we can manage nicely with this tree. Now,' she added briskly, 'what do we do for decorations?'

Susan looked blankly at her. 'I assumed that you had some.'

'Well, this family has never thrown out anything, so there must be all kinds of things somewhere. Randy, go and ask Vera if she knows where the Christmas things are stored. Susan and Ronnie can go with you and pick out what they want. No sense in hauling all that junk in here to the living-room.'

Ronnie and Susan were ecstatic when they saw the piles of furniture, old clothes, books and toys scattered about the dark, lofty attic where Vera sent them. Randy finally succeeded in dragging them to the boxes of Christmas decorations, and with great difficulty, kept them to their chore of selecting what they wanted. Their choices made, burdened with treasures, they descended once more to the living-room. Elizabeth was pleased with their selections, and they gaily decorated the tree, all laughing as

Elizabeth and Randy, prompted by the old, familiar decorations, dredged up old memories about past Christmases.

Susan sat back on her heels and looked about the comfortable living-room. In earlier days the large room with its high ceiling, tall windows and distinct mouldings would have been called the parlour. Over the years the Gerard family had stamped its own personality on the room, and only the deep wine-coloured velvet curtains showed the Victorian influence. Modern leather loungers mixed freely with gay chintz sofas draped with patchwork quilts. Computer magazines and ranching journals shared a side table with an abandoned stetson hat. The old-fashioned marble fireplace boasted a huge crackling fire, but glass doors prevented the room's warm air from escaping up the chimney. This was a room that had survived generations of cowboy boots, pets and children, and now it took the scrawny, lopsided tree in its stride. She looked the tree over critically. 'Well?' she challenged her decoration partners. 'What do you think now?'

'You've done a magnificent job of disguise,' said Elizabeth tactfully.

'It's not half bad,' Randy admitted. 'Provided , of course, you can persuade everyone to stand directly in front of the tree so they don't see how it leans forward or notice the gaps at the back.'

Susan stuck out her tongue at Randy, and turned to Ronnie. 'What do you think?'

Ronnie giggled. 'I love it. I can hardly wait for Burke to see it.'

Randy turned his head towards the window.

'Speak of the devil—I thought I just heard him and your mom come in.'

'Randy, let's turn off the room lights and turn on the tree lights and surprise them.' Ronnie jumped up and down in her excitement.

'Okay, kid. Run and hit the light switch when I say to. I'll just crawl under the tree and plug in the cord.'

In her excitement, Ronnie failed to listen to Randy, and she ran eagerly to the switch and immediately plunged the room into darkness.

'Hey, not yet!' Randy's muffled howl sounded from beneath the tree. 'I can't find the wall outlet.'

Susan tried not to laugh as she heard the swishing of branches and several soft plops as Randy brushed the tree, knocking ornaments on to the floor. At least nothing sounded as if it broke.

Voices could be heard in the hall. Suddenly Susan doubted her wisdom in selecting a tree that everyone insisted that Burke would not like. Had she deliberately tried to irritate him again in retribution for his calling her a shrew? No. She had long hated the practice of cutting down perfect trees, while leaving the weak and ugly to proliferate. The question was, how would Burke view her actions? She felt herself grow cold.

Footsteps paused in the doorway, and the room was flooded with light at the same time that Randy found the wall socket and plugged in the tree lights. Susan's eyes flew to Burke standing stock-still in the doorway, his eyes riveted on the Christmas tree. An astonished Tiffany stood behind him. No one uttered a sound. Susan looked around and wondered if her own face mirrored the guilty expressions etched on everyone else's face.

Randy backed out from beneath the tree, saying, 'Next time wait until I say, "okay", Ronnie. Now you can turn off the lights.'

'Too late,' Susan said as she tried not to laugh at the astonished faces of the couple who remained speechless in the doorway.

Randy, still crouched on all fours, turned his head to look at Susan. 'What do you mean, too late?'

She nodded towards the door, and Randy's head swivelled about. 'Oh,' he said sheepishly as he spied his brother. 'Hi.'

Burke slowly advanced into the room. 'You all look like you've been caught stealing the family silver,' he observed. As he walked closer to the tree, his eyes widened, and he looked incredulously at Randy. Slowly he walked from one side of the tree to the other, peering closely at the branches. Once he reached in and tested a limb that Randy had wired in place.

Susan held her breath, as she felt everyone else was doing, awaiting Burke's judgment. He stood, his back to the room, and said nothing. Susan saw his shoulders begin to tremble and then shake violently.

'Burke?' Elizabeth questioned quietly.

He wheeled to face his mother, and it was immediately apparent to everyone that he was fighting a losing battle with amusement. The silent chuckles gave way to booming laughter. Gradually the silence of the room penetrated his mirth, and he worked at bringing his laughter under control. 'Where in God's name did you find that—that misbegotten excuse for a tree?'

Randy squirmed under Burke's quizzical interrogation. Susan could see he was torn between loyalty

he agreed, as she rewarded him with a moist kiss and a tight hug.

Elizabeth stood up and smiled at Ronnie. 'Now that we have our tree up, what we need are packages under it. Do you suppose you could help me carry some from my room?'

The little girl eagerly assented, and the two left the room, with Tiffany drifting out after them. Randy gathered up his tools, and with an awkward grin at Burke, followed them. Having no desire to be left with Burke, Susan edged towards the door.

Before she could reach it and the safety it promised, Burke grabbed her arm and held her captive. 'Stay a minute. I want to talk to you.'

Susan had not forgiven him for calling her a shrew. 'I'm busy.'

'This will only take a minute. I want to apologise.'

'For calling me a shrew? I couldn't care less what you think of me!'

'For laughing at your tree,' he corrected her.

Susan averted her eyes to avoid the laughter gleaming in his. 'I don't care if you don't like it,' she said stiffly.

'I've changed my mind. I do like it. At least,' he corrected himself after looking at the tree and shuddering dramatically, 'I like the effect of the tree. As Ronnie said, it makes everyone laugh. I don't think I've seen Tiffany smile like that since Steve died. I've watched you with both her and Ronnie. You're good for them. You've pepped them up. Tiffany, especially, has been moping around too much.'

'Burke!' Susan was aghast. 'She's just lost her husband!'

'It's been almost two years,' he reminded her. 'I don't expect her to wash Steve totally out of her life, but I do think it's time she got back to the business of living. She's still a young woman.' He paused before adding abruptly, 'She ought to remarry.' Jamming his hands into his pockets, he paced around the room. 'If I could only be sure how she felt,' he said, almost to himself. He narrowed his eyes in speculation at Susan. 'I don't suppose she's said anything to you?'

'No. That is, about what?' she faltered.

'Getting married again. Isn't that what we're talking about?' he asked in exasperation.

'That's what you're talking about,' answered Susan curtly. 'I don't think Tiffany's plans are any of my business.'

Burke snorted. 'I doubt that.' He took another turn around the room. 'Tiffany's never had many female friends, but she likes you and talks to you.'

'So?' Susan didn't like the thoughtful look on Burke's face.

'You could give her a little shove. As a teacher, point out how Ronnie needs a father.'

'I will not! Do your own persuading.'

'I might have known you'd put a spoke in my wheel,' said Burke in disgust. 'How can you be around Tif for more than five seconds and not realise that she needs to have a man around? Don't make the mistake of thinking that just because you don't, no woman does.'

Susan stiffened. 'A woman doesn't marry to provide a father for her child or to have someone handy to change the lightbulbs,' she said indignantly. 'There's a little thing called love.'

'Is that why you've never married?'

'You needn't say it like I'm ninety years old. I'm only twenty-four,' Susan said tartly.

'You didn't answer my question,' he persisted.

She raised her chin. 'Not that it's any of your business, but yes, I'm holding out for love. What did you think?'

'That you don't need a man, that you intend to prove that men are superfluous to your life.'

'I don't know where you got that idea.'

'Maybe when you made it so very clear that you'd accept no favours from me the night we met—including a helping hand up when you fell.'

'Oh.' Susan reddened. 'That was just because I was so angry with you.'

'With me? I didn't run into you.'

'No, but you snarled and roared at me. Then you walked off and left me.'

'Your choice.'

'No gentleman would have left me stranded like that.'

'You know darn well you were prepared to stand there and argue all night with me. If I hadn't walked off, we'd still be standing there fighting.'

Refusing to dignify his accusation with a denial, Susan continued, 'You were an unfeeling brute when I was cold and tired.'

'You were so miserable that if I'd said three kind words in a row to you, you'd have sat down in the road and cried.'

'I would not have!'

'We'll never know, will we?' He grinned unexpectedly. 'Every time I think about how determined you were not to give me the satisfaction of knowing how much you hated that stinking horse blanket . . .' His eyes danced with laughter.

'I'm glad you were so amused,' Susan said, trying to ignore the dip her stomach had taken at the winsome look on Burke's face. It was crazy the way her pulse was affected by a man she didn't even like. Breathlessly she turned the subject. 'I thought we were talking about Tiffany needing to get married, not me.'

Her words wiped the laughter from Burke's face, and his eyes narrowed to dark slits. 'We were, weren't we?' He turned away. 'As you were so quick to point out, Tiffany isn't your problem.'

'I didn't mean that,' she denied hastily. 'I just think you're worrying too much. She just needs time.'

'Maybe you're right.' He started towards the hall. At the door, he turned for one parting look at the tree. 'The more I look at that, the more I can see it's exactly the type of tree you would choose.'

'What's that supposed to mean?' Susan was instantly suspicious.

Burke chuckled. 'Figure it out yourself,' he retorted. 'You're the teacher.' He strolled from the room, leaving behind a fuming Susan.

CHAPTER FIVE

As it turned out, Tiffany was the one who brought up
the subject of her remarriage the next day.

'Am I interrupting a great story?'

Susan set aside the book she'd been reading. 'As a
matter of fact, this book is so boring that any
interruption is welcome.' Elizabeth had decided to
lie down to rest for a while and, knowing Tiffany and
Ronnie were wrapping gifts, Susan had been
reluctant to disturb them. Now she smiled with
pleasure at Tiffany. The dark-haired woman was
dressed in a stunning trouser suit, the emerald-green
colour a vivid backdrop for her exotic beauty.

'I want to thank you for being so good to Ronnie.
She's fallen in love with you,' she said.

'She's an easy child to be good to. You've done a
marvellous job of raising her.'

'Sometimes I don't think I had a thing to do with
how she is. She was so good and happy, even as a
baby. And I know that I've neglected her at times.
Especially after Steven died. I was so caught up in
my own loss, I forgot what Ronnie must be suffering.
Burke came out and saw in a glance what was
happening. He really raked me over the coals for
being so selfish. I cried for days.'

Susan was indignant at Burke's lack of compassion. 'You shouldn't let him get away with pushing
you around like that. He's a born bully.'

'No, no; he was right. Every time Ronnie tried to

talk to me about how sad she felt, I changed the
subject or hushed her up because it was so painful for
me. Poor little girl. I forgot that she needed to grieve,
too.'

'What's done is done,' Susan said briskly. 'You've
got all of Ronnie's future in which to make up for any
omissions of the past.'

Tiffany strolled over to the window where she
brushed her fingertips along the sill. 'I've been told
that I ought to get remarried for Ronnie's sake. What
do you think?'

'I think that's a stupid reason to get married,'
Susan said bluntly, casting Burke into imaginary
perdition. She should have known he'd never listen
to any advice of hers. 'Tell him to mind his own
business, and you'll get married when you want
to . . .' Her voice trailed off at the dreamy expression
on Tiffany's face. 'You do want to,' she guessed.

Tiffany whirled around, the dreamy expression
replaced by one of uncertainty. 'I think so. That is,
he did tell me I should get married, but he . . . well
. . . he hasn't proposed. I've given him every
opportunity.' She sniffed. 'Maybe it's all in my
imagination. Maybe he's just not interested.'

'I'm sure he is,' Susan said soothingly. Should she
tell Tiffany that Burke had tried to talk her into
pushing the other woman into his arms?

'I'm not so young any more, almost thirty.
Although that's not too old to have children. He's
wonderful with Ronnie, but he deserves to have
sons, tall and proud like he is.' Glumly Tiffany
added, 'Too proud.'

Susan had no difficulty in translating the cryptic
remark. After all, Tiffany had jilted Burke once.

Pride wouldn't allow him to lay himself open to rejection again. This time Tiffany would have to do the pursuing. She attempted to put her thoughts into words. 'Perhaps you ought to ask him to marry you.'

'I couldn't do that. What if he said no?'

'Isn't it worth the risk? He might say yes. I think it's time you stood up and fought for your own happiness. You can't spend the rest of your life letting other people decide what you want to do,' she pointed out gently.

Tiffany smiled wanly. 'I'll think about it,' she promised. Pausing as she left the room, she added, 'I wish I was more like you. You know what you want, and you don't let anyone stop you getting it.'

Once that might have been true, Susan thought wryly. But ever since she had met Elizabeth, her whole world seemed to have been tossed topsy-turvy. She ought to feel happiness for Tiffany, not this jealousy eating away at her insides. She wasn't jealous because Burke loved Tiffany, it was just that—well, it might be nice to be a Tiffany. A woman whom men took care of and cosseted. Burke would never shout at Tiffany or expect her to tramp miles in the cold and snow. He would see to her wellbeing, make sure that she had what she wanted without ever asking her and do all in his power to protect her from the vagaries of life. Susan caught herself short. She was describing her brothers' care for her, a smothering love that she had fought against all her life. Was that something to yearn for? No, of course not. Then why did she feel so discontented? She must be having holiday blues. Casting aside the boring book, she decided she would go and see if Ronnie wanted to go outside and play. A romp in the snow would cheer her up.

Pensively she crossed the large entry hall, her footsteps alternately loud on the wooden parquet floor and soft as she stepped on the small gleaming Oriental rugs scattered about. A loud swishing sound cut into her melancholy thoughts, and she quickly halted and looked up.

Randy was swooping backwards down the stair railing, his long legs astride the banister. Heart caught in her throat, she watched him land with a graceful thud at the bottom, his back to Susan.

'Well,' she said with mock sternness, 'no wonder there's no finial at the bottom!'

Startled, Randy turned and shot her a shamefaced grin. 'It's been missing for years. Dad said he used to come down the same way when he was a kid. Mom's not the first mother who's threatened to replace it. She says when we grow up, she will,' he added.

'Judging by present behaviour, I'd say she still has quite a wait,' said Susan drily.

'You're just jealous because you're too old and afraid to do it,' Randy jeered.

'I am not!'

'Sure you are. I dare you to try it.'

Challenged, Susan refused to back away. 'All right. You wait right here.' She ran swiftly up the stairs. Halfway up she stopped and turning to Randy, asked, in what she hoped was an unconcerned voice, 'How do you know when you're at the bottom?'

'Practice.'

'Oh.' Susan bit her lip in indecision.

'Come on, Susan.' Randy grinned boyishly. 'I'll catch you before you can fly off.'

'Promise?'

'Cross my heart and hope to die,' he said solemnly, matching actions to words.

Reassured, Susan ran lightly to the top of the stairs and straddled the banister, her back to Randy. 'Ready or not, here I come,' she chanted. Her hands were warmed by friction and the pictures on the wall flashed by as she careened in dizzying descent. At the bottom she flew into space and knew a moment of panic before strong arms caught her and held her close. Randy's beating heart sounded a thunderous counterpoint to her own.

'That was fun, Randy. Wait a minute—I want to do it again.' She turned and looked, not into Randy's laughing face, but into Burke's set white countenance with darkened grey eyes blazing down at her.

'What kind of stupid trick was that? Are you trying to kill yourself?'

He continued to hold her off the ground, and Susan struggled to free herself. 'Put me down right this instant!'

His immediate compliance was unexpected, and she landed awkwardly and had to grasp his arm to maintain her balance. Burke continued to stare angrily at her.

'Where's ... where's Randy?' she managed to stutter.

'He's gone,' Burke said coldly. 'There's some excuse for him, he's still a kid, but you ought to know better than to try a hare-brained stunt like that. One expects a teacher to have a few grains of good sense!'

'Oh pooh,' scoffed Susan airily, delighted to see that her cavalier attitude further enraged Burke. 'Just because you're too old to have fun any more.'

She unconsciously parroted Randy's taunt, even as she was guiltily aware that Burke's anger had its roots in his fear for her.

'Is that so?' Burke demanded furiously as he disengaged her hand which was still, to her mortification, clutching his arm, and stamped up the stairs.

Susan stood hesitantly at the bottom of the staircase. It wasn't like Burke to walk off, letting her have the last word.

'Get out of the way!' he cried, and Susan stepped aside in the nick of time as he flew down the banister and landed nimbly on his feet before her. He turned around, hands on hips, eyes glaring at her. 'Too old, am I?' he demanded.

Susan's mouth quivered, and she bit her lip, but she was unable to keep her laughter from spilling out.

Burke glared at her, and then reluctantly a smile tugged at the corners of his lips, and he grinned ruefully at her. 'I never could resist a challenge,' he admitted.

'I've never been so surprised in my life! The idea of you sliding down banisters.' She giggled again at the memory. 'The last person on earth . . .' she began.

'Obviously you don't know me as well as you think you do,' Burke interrupted. His hands rested on her shoulders as he faced her.

'Obviously,' Susan retorted.

'We should remedy that.' He pulled her closer and tipped her chin up with a closed fist. 'One should always know one's enemy.' His face descended towards her, eyes narrowed, watching for her reaction.

She dropped her eyelids, but his face was imprinted on her brain. Those devastatingly attractive crinkly lines about his eyes, the deep wrinkles like a gash beside his mouth.

His mouth. Lightly, gently, he kissed her, and she relived her careening ride down the banister. She clutched at his shirt to push him away, give herself support, or pull him nearer—she hardly knew which. Feelings she had never experienced raced through her body as he nibbled, teased and slowly, yet inexorably, parted her lips with his own. When he tugged her closer to his muscled form, she went willingly. She felt his warm hands on her hips, the anchor that kept her from being flung into space as again and again they rode in dizzying climb and descent. She felt his tongue leisurely investigating the hidden recesses of her mouth. Curiously, hesitantly, she touched her own tongue to his. He became still and passive, and boldly she explored the newness of the sensations that poured over her. At last, satisfied, she began to withdraw. Instantly, he captured her head, his large hands thrust through her hair and holding her lips firm against his. Now it was he who took the lead again, demanding that she follow him on a trip to regions she'd never dreamed of. She went spinning off into dazzling space.

'Why are you kissing each other?'

Susan fell back to earth with a thud. She sprang back from Burke. Ronnie stood halfway down the staircase regarding them with intense interest. Susan tried to move further away from Burke, but his arm held her entrapped at his side.

'Men like to kiss pretty women,' Burke answered.

'Daddy was always kissing Mama. Do you think that's why she cries sometimes at night? Because she doesn't have anybody to kiss her?'

'I'm sure your mother misses your daddy very much,' Burke answered soberly, leaving Susan's side. Catching Ronnie up in his arms, he sat on the lower step, gently cradling his small burden in his arms.

Cuddled trustingly against Burke's chest, Ronnie said sadly, 'I miss my daddy, too. I wish he didn't have to go away. Mama said God needed him, but Mama and I need him real bad, Burke.'

'I know, sweetheart.' Over Ronnie's head he threw Susan a silent plea for help, as the small girl sniffed.

She sat down beside them, but left Ronnie in Burke's arms. Burke was the best medicine for Ronnie, holding her and giving her comfort. He was so good with Ronnie, and it was obvious that she adored him. There was no doubt in Susan's mind that Burke would make Ronnie an excellent stepfather. And father. Tiffany was set on giving him sons. The photo of Burke as a child flashed across her mind, and she knew that any sons of his were bound to be sturdy and robust. And probably cocky as well, she added to herself. Tiffany would have her hands full controlling that family of males. *She* could control Burke's sons. A firm hand and a loving heart was all they needed. Now where did those outrageous thoughts come from?

Ronnie sat up, drying her eyes. 'I'm sorry I cried, Burke,' she said softly.

'It's okay to cry when you feel bad. Don't ever feel sorry about missing your daddy, honey. I miss him, too. Any time you want someone to talk to about your daddy, you come to me, okay?'

Ronnie nodded, her eyes still bright with unshed tears. Shyly she threw her arms around Burke. 'I love you.'

Burke hugged the little body so trustingly curled in his lap. 'I love you, too, sweetheart.' He cleared his throat. 'Now that we have it settled that we're a mutual admiration society, why . . .'

'What's a mutual admir . . . whatever you said?' the child asked, screwing her pixie face up in perplexity.

'A mutual admiration society?' In answer to her nod, he explained, 'It's a group of people who like each other.'

'Oh.' A thought struck her. 'Can anybody join? Like a club?'

'Well, I suppose so. I hadn't thought about it. Why? Do you want someone else in our society?'

Ronnie nodded her head decisively. 'Susan. She's so nice and pretty.'

Startled hazel eyes met cool grey. 'Would you care to join our mutual admiration society, Miss Osborne?'

The thread of mockery in Burke's voice reminded Susan that he had just called them enemies. Ignoring him, she turned to Ronnie. 'Thank you very much, Miss Tallerton. I'd be honoured.'

'That's settled then.' Burke stood up, gently setting Ronnie on her feet. 'Now, who wants to ride into Castle Rock with me to buy some supplies?'

'I do! I do!' Ronnie hopped up and down in her excitement.

'Susan?'

Before she could turn down the invitation her presence forced him to issue, Ronnie interceded.

'Please come, Susan,' she pleaded. 'Burke goes in a store and people stop to talk to him, and they talk and talk and talk . . .'

'Okay,' Susan laughed, 'I get the picture. You want to go and I'm supposed to come along to save you from possible boredom.'

Ronnie wasn't sure what possible boredom was, but she knew when she'd won, so she raced upstairs to inform her mother of the treat in store.

'Susan.' Burke's deep tones prevented Susan from following the small girl. 'Thanks.'

'Thanks? But I didn't do anything.'

'You stayed and kept us company. Most people would have been so embarrassed when Ronnie broke down that they would have made some excuse and left or else tried to cheer her up.'

'I couldn't have done that. Then Ronnie would have thought grieving for her father was wrong.' Honesty forced her to add, 'You were wonderful with her.'

'Surprises you, doesn't it,' he mocked.

'Yes,' she snapped. Couldn't he even be gracious about accepting a compliment?

Burke shook his head. 'Temper, temper. You really should have red hair.'

Irritated that he'd once again managed to get under her skin, Susan blurted out the first thought that entered her mind. 'Tiffany is crazy to want to marry an arrogant beast like you!'

'What?' He shot the word at her.

Susan was appalled that she had violated Tiffany's confidences. 'I shouldn't have said anything.'

Burke gripped her arm compellingly. 'Well, you did. Now finish it.'

'Tiffany,' she faltered, 'Tiffany talked to me about . . . about what you said yesterday. I . . . I think she's considering remarriage. It . . . it may be that she's gathering her courage.'

'She said my name?' Burke was relentless.

'Yes—no—I don't know. Who else would she be talking about?' she cried.

Burke stared at her, an arrested look in his eyes. 'Who else indeed?'

Without answering, she turned and went up the stairs.

Burke shouted after her, 'Fifteen minutes!'

'What?' she stopped and turned halfway up the stairs.

'Be ready to leave in fifteen minutes. Oh, and Susan,' he added provocatively, 'any time you want to slide down the banister, just let me know.' The memory of grey eyes brimming with amusement followed her up the stairs.

Standing in front of her mirror, she wrenched a comb through her hair. Men like to kiss pretty girls. Burke's words to Ronnie ran round and around inside her head. He hadn't been answering Ronnie's question as much as he'd been sending a message to Susan that she shouldn't take his kisses seriously. Burke wasn't about to surrender tamely to Tiffany after her treatment of him. Who could blame him if he played hard to get, and at the same time amused himself with his mother's houseguest? How could she have kissed Burke like that, forgetting all about Tiffany? She slammed her comb down on the dressing table. Burke could just find someone else to play his kissing games with.

One of the ranch wagons was parked in front of the house, but there was no sign of Burke or Ronnie when Susan arrived outside, breathless from her hurried preparations. No smog marred the perfect day, giving Susan a magnificent view of the distant Rockies, the snow-covered peaks stark against the clear blue sky. White fluffy clouds flirted with danger, daring the ragged peaks to rip them apart. Nearer to her, scrub oak and scrawny pines dotted the rolling hills. Leaning against the front of the pick-up, she studied the front view of the large, imposing Gerard home. Round roofs, peaked eaves and fanciful wood trim all spoke of the Victorian influence, and lent the house a bold vitality not often associated with ranch homes.

'Not what one expects way out here, is it?'

Burke's deep voice gave Susan a start. 'I must admit it gave me quite a shock the first time I saw it in the daylight. A Victorian mansion lording it over the rural countryside must be a little unusual.'

'The house takes a little getting used to. The Gerard who built it in the mid-1880s was a miner who found his mother lode, and then became an honest-to-goodness cattle baron. When he decided to marry, he went up to Denver, looked around at what was being built and brought back an architect who designed and built this home for the new bride. Fortunately, before he could get carried away inside, his more practical bride was able to insist more on comfort than fanciful ornamentation. He did manage to sneak in a few Victorian touches, however.'

If Susan hadn't been studying the ornate iron finial which topped the highest tower of the house, she would have thought before she said absently, 'The staircase must be one of his touches.'

'I believe it was. Luckily for me.'

Ronnie's excited arrival at the truck gave Susan an excuse to ignore Burke's provocative remark. Wordlessly she obeyed his injunction to buckle up, and the pick-up took off with a roar. Burke was obviously in a good mood, and it was a beautiful day. The best thing to do was just to sit back and enjoy the outing.

Her decision made, she looked out of the window to enjoy the passing landscape. Small grey birds, the kind that Elizabeth had called snowbirds, flashed up from the edge of the road as they passed. Here and there rough tracks slashed through the land, and huge boulders and rocky pinnacles thrust themselves into the blue sky. As they were travelling west, the Rockies loomed larger and larger, with the flat land becoming rolling hills. Fences paralleling the road were heaped with giant tumbleweeds and odd bits of rubbish testifying to the wind that occasionally swept down through the hills. Lone trees dotted the landscape, while a solitary windmill stood sentinel against the sky. Susan was about to interrupt Burke's teasing conversation with Ronnie to ask how far to town when she was diverted by a flash of white to her right. As she watched, about a dozen animals bounded into view, their rumps shining white in the morning sun.

'Burke, look. Are those antelope?'

Burke squinted in the direction of her pointing finger, and slowed the pick-up to a stop. 'Well, you can call them that. Everyone does, but actually they're not true antelope and should be called pronghorns.'

'Whatever they're called, they're beautiful.'

'Where are they?' Ronnie bounced impatiently up and down on the seat.

As Burke directed the small girl's attention in the right direction, the animals paused on a high knoll, looking back towards the truck. Smaller than most deer, their distinctive brown and white coat was a perfect camouflage against the sage-covered landscape.

'Why don't they run?' asked Susan, puzzled at the pronghorns' behaviour.

'They're about the most curious animals around. They're just as interested in you as you are in them. That's frequently their downfall. Many a handsome buck has lost his life because he went to investigate a handkerchief stuck on a pole by an enterprising hunter.'

'That doesn't seem fair. Is that why there aren't any males in this group?'

'There's a male up there,' Burke countered. 'See that big guy with black on his face and down the side of his neck? He's a male.'

'What's a male, Burke?' Ronnie asked curiously.

'A daddy pronghorn.'

'Susan is right, Burke. There can't be any daddys up there. None of them have any horns.'

'She's right. None of them have antlers,' Susan agreed with Ronnie.

'Talk about a couple of city slickers,' Burke teased. 'Pronghorns don't have antlers, they have horns. What's more, frequently even the females have horns. All of them, however, lose their horns at the end of the breeding season, and this guy has already shed his. He'll grow them back in time for the mating season late next summer. He'll need them then to fight off all the other bucks who'd like to steal his harem.'

The buck stood at rigid attention on the top of the rise, still intent on the truck, curiosity and caution obviously warring within him. Suddenly, caution seemed to win, and with an almost contemptuous flash of the white hairs on his rump, the larger animal sprang away, the other pronghorns bounding in his wake; in seconds, the landscape was once again barren of visible life.

'What scared them, Burke? Will they come back?' Ronnie's disappointment was clearly marked in her voice.

'It's hard to say what scared them. Keep an eye peeled, and you might see more. There aren't as many of them roaming around as there used to be, but we still have plenty,' he consoled her as he started up the car.

Like Ronnie, Susan was silent during the rest of the trip, scanning the landscape in the hope of sighting more of the beautiful wild creatures. In her mind she could still see the magnificent buck as he had regally surveyed his surroundings. For some reason, the buck reminded her of a picture of Burke that Elizabeth had shown her. The picture was of him astride a large stallion, his face alert and watchful, intent on something in the distance. There was about the two the same air of command and masculine arrogance ... the buck with his harem, and Burke, she had no doubt, with his.

In town, Burke dropped Susan and Ronnie off in the middle of the old section where interesting shops vied with each other for the passers-by's attention.

The two were quite content to browse their way up and down the street, exclaiming over the inexpensive as well as the expensive from the various craft and gift stores. When an intricately carved bird feeder decorated with the image of St Francis of Assisi caught her eye, Susan could not resist buying it for Elizabeth in spite of the fact that she already had a Christmas present for the older woman. The time allotted to them by Burke passed before they realised it, and Susan was chagrined to look down at her watch and see that unless they hurried very fast, Burke was going to be impatiently waiting for them at their designated meeting place. Awkwardly carrying the bulky package, she hustled Ronnie down the street, oblivious to the other's protests.

'Burke won't be there,' the child insisted. 'People always stop and talk to him, and then he can't get away.'

While not doubting the truth of Ronnie's statement, Susan was determined not to make Burke wait for her. Therefore it was a great relief when the place for their appointed rendezvous came in to view, and there was no sign of a huge, irate, pacing male. Slowing to a more moderate pace, she silently thanked whoever had held Burke up this time. A particularly busy street ran just ahead of them, and Susan took Ronnie's hand preparatory to crossing. Unfortunately at that same moment, the obstreperous package began to slip, and comic farce ensued as Susan attempted to regain control of it as well as her wayward purse, all without relinquishing Ronnie's hand. Ronnie's efforts to help spurred the package on to greater effort to escape. Just as it made a successful bid for freedom, and Susan foresaw

Elizabeth's gift becoming nothing more than splinters, an enormous grey-clad arm reached around her and grabbed the package seconds before it smashed to the cement. She looked up to see a large, red-faced man grinning down at her from beneath an enormous stetson.

'Looked like you needed a little help lassoing that maverick,' he boomed.

'I certainly did,' she agreed, still breathless from her struggles. 'Thank you so much for your help.'

'Always willing to help a pretty filly, ma'am.' He tipped his cowboy hat. 'The name is Webb— Howard Webb. Saw you earlier when you got out of Burke's truck. Leave it to Burke; he always corrals the pretty ones!'

Almost overwhelmed by the man's exuberance, Susan smiled weakly. 'Do you ranch around here also, Mr Webb?'

'Dear me, no, honey. I'm a banker.'

'A banker?' she repeated incredulously.

'Sure 'nuf. That's how I met old Burke there, and your daddy, too, as far as that goes.'

'My daddy?' she echoed weakly.

'Why, I knew you were Senator Payton's daughter the minute you stepped out of Burke's truck. Betting's been high around here that Burke wouldn't let some polecat rustle you out from under his eyes this time around. Now that I see you, I can understand what all the shouting's about.'

'I think there's some mistake, Mr Webb.'

'Susan.' Ronnie tugged on her hand. Ignoring the adult conversation, she had been watching the street. 'Here comes Burke now.'

Embarrassment turned Susan's face a bright red.

She had to extricate herself from this situation before Burke reached them. 'Mr Webb——'

'Oh, call me Howard. Everybody around here does.'

'Howard, then. I believe you're under the misapprehension that I'm Tiffany Tallerton. The truth is . . .'

'Burke, you ol' coyote, how ya been?'

'Fine, Howard, and you?'

Susan bit her lip as the two men, plainly good friends, shook hands. With luck, Howard Webb would not repeat his mistake to Burke. At his next words, she sighed. She should have known better.

'Why I was just saying to Mrs Tallerton here . . .'

'Mrs Tallerton?' Burke turned to Susan, his right eyebrow arched quizzically.

'I've been trying to explain to Mr Webb . . . Howard,' she gritted her teeth at the interruption, 'that I'm not Tiffany.'

'You're not? Why, I could have sworn this little lady here was calling Senator Payton "Grandpa" the last time I saw her.'

At Susan's silent plea for help, Burke attempted to explain. 'That's correct, Howard. This is Ronnie Tallerton,' he indicated the girl whose hand was linked with his, 'her companion, however, is Susan Osborne, a friend of Elizabeth's from Denver who is spending the holidays with us.'

Howard's red face turned even redder, if possible. 'And to think that I thought you were Mrs Tallerton! I apologise, Miss Osborne. When Burke showed up with a lovely lady in tow, with word around that Mrs Tallerton was back in town, I naturally assumed . . .'

'That I was she,' Susan finished for him.

'I sure am sorry.'

Howard's visible embarrassment combined with his need continuously and profusely to apologise to Susan quickly made her extremely uncomfortable, and she was thankful when Burke swiftly and easily terminated the conversation, leading her and Ronnie back to the truck.

Driving back to the ranch, Burke failed to allude to the conversation, but one point was driving Susan crazy. 'I don't see how Mr Webb could mistake me for Tiffany when they've both lived here all their lives. The community isn't that large.'

Burke laughed out loud. 'Howard, a native? Good lord, no. He grew up in New York City.'

'New York?' Susan thought of the cowboy boots peeping from beneath the tailored suit, the bolo tie with its huge turquoise stone. 'You've got to be kidding!'

'Nope. He moved out here a few years ago when his company bought into a local bank and appointed him to manage it.'

Susan giggled. 'I think he's more western than Roy Rogers.'

'Funny you should say that. He has a palomino horse named Trigger.'

'You're making that up!'

'You're right, I am. I just like to hear you laugh.'

'Susan does have a pretty laugh, doesn't she, Burke?' Ronnie's entry into the conversation spared Susan from having to reply to Burke's surprising comment. 'Mama said listening to Susan is like listening to a mountain stream. I'm not sure what Mama meant, but I do like to listen to Susan. She reads to me, you know.'

'No, I didn't know. Do you like that?'

'Yes. Mama doesn't like to read to me. She says she can't sit still that long. Mama doesn't have a nice voice like Susan, but she is awful pretty, isn't she?' The small child looked artlessly up at Susan.

'Your mama is very pretty,' Susan agreed.

'Of course, you're pretty, too, Susan,' Ronnie rushed to add.

'Thank you very much. I think that you're pretty as well.' Ronnie shook her head. 'No curls,' she explained succinctly.

Susan looked helplessly at Burke.

'Hey, are you saying bad things about my favourite girl-friend?' he asked in mock fierceness.

'Am I your favourite girl-friend, Burke?' asked Ronnie wistfully.

'Didn't I give you my dessert last night at dinner?' he demanded.

Ronnie laughed and rubbed her cheek against Burke's arm. 'I love you.'

'I suppose that means you want my dessert tonight, too,' he teased.

Concentrating on the landscape outside the windows, Susan winked away incipient tears. The warm relationship that Ronnie and Burke enjoyed tugged at her heartstrings. Ronnie obviously trusted Burke very much to be so honest and open about her emotions with him. Not all adults could establish that kind of rapport with a small child. It was forcing Susan to view Burke from another angle.

Inside the truck there was silence. Ronnie soon grew drowsy, and at Susan's suggestion, lay down, her head resting in Susan's lap, and was soon fast asleep. Brushing back the hair from Ronnie's forehead, Susan looked up to see Burke watching her, an odd expression on his face.

'You're good with kids,' he said brusquely.

Susan shrugged off the compliment. 'That's my job.'

'I have to admit that I was surprised when Elizabeth told me you taught kindergarten.'

'Why?'

'Oh, I don't know.' His attention returned to the road. 'From our encounters, limited as they were, I would have expected you to be a person who'd go in for real teaching, like in high school or college.'

Ronnie's sleeping presence forced Susan to swallow her irritation at Burke's provocative remark. She had to content herself with remarking quietly, 'That's an ignorant idea that is, unfortunately shared by too many parents who feel that kindergarten just doesn't count. On the contrary, the first year of infants is the most important year of a child's school career.'

'I'll concede important, but most important? Learning to tie your shoes?' he scoffed.

'Kindergarten today is more than learning how to tie your shoes, or naming colours, or saying the alphabet. Of course, we do that, too,' she hastened to add, 'but so many of our activities deal with reading readiness and number awareness, not to mention social and physical development.'

'You mean, now it's all down to business, and no hugging or reading of stories?'

'Certainly not. Hugging is just as important as ever, maybe more so with so many single parents and working mothers. As for reading, the more we read to children, the more anxious they are to read themselves.'

'Sounds like a lot of work.'

'Maybe to some people. To me it's a challenge, and the rewards are tremendous. To see the look of satisfaction on a face when little fingers successfully complete a puzzle, or to watch two children work out how they can both use the same toy either by playing together or taking turns, or to see the delight of a child when he or she recognises a written word for the first time——' She stopped her flow of words abruptly. 'Sorry. I guess I tend to get a little carried away. It's just that kindergarten is so important. The rest of a child's school career is influenced by that year. Besides,' she returned to his statement, 'what you do for a living is a lot of work. Do you like it the less for that?'

'*Touché*. You must have been on the school debating team. To answer your question: yes, running the ranch and the business is a lot of work, and yes, I enjoy every minute of it. I didn't at first, I have to admit. I suppose that Elizabeth's told you about Dad dying and leaving things in rather a mess.' At her nod, he continued, 'There were times when I was so angry at the fates for taking him and leaving everything for me to straighten out. A couple of times I even found myself hating Dad for dumping all his responsibilities in my lap.'

'I think anger at a person who died happens to all of us.'

'That's right. Your parents are dead, too.'

'Yes, when I was much younger. But I had people who cared for me, not the other way around.' She was curious. 'What did you plan to do?'

'You'll laugh. I wanted to be a veterinarian.'

Remembering his tenderness and concern for Ronnie, and having seen the way he cared for his livestock, Susan was sure he would have been a good one. 'Are you sorry that you didn't get to become a vet? Do you still hate the ranching?'

'You know, it's a funny thing. I'd make a goal, and say that as soon as I reached it, I would turn things over to someone else, and go back to vet school. Then, that goal attained, something else would come up. One day it finally occurred to me that I really loved ranching and the business. It was a challenge that I thrived on, and we began to branch out. Now the Gerard empire, so to speak, encompasses not only the beef operation, but we have interests in gold and mineral developments all over the state, not to mention investments in real estate in Denver.' He glanced over at Susan. 'It probably sounds like I'm bragging.'

'No,' she said slowly. 'I think a person should be enthused by his work. If not, perhaps he ought to try a different career. In fact, that's why I think . . .' Her voice trailed off as she realised the direction of her words.

'Why you think I ought to let Randy make up his own mind,' Burke finished her sentence.

She nodded her head defiantly.

'You could be right.'

'Oh, no! Don't agree with me,' Susan mocked. 'You'll ruin your reputation.'

'Don't take it to heart,' said Burke drily. 'It'll probably never happen again.' Signalling that their conversation was over, he began to whistle a popular country tune, tapping his fingers on the steering wheel in time with the catchy melody.

Ronnie continued to sleep, and the remainder of the ride back to the ranch was accomplished without conversation. Susan was glad of the silence, as the day's events had given her a great deal to think about. Burke was turning out to be a much more complex person that she had supposed him to be. She was already aware that he was greatly respected by his ranch personnel, and now, if this Howard Webb were any indication, his friends and neighbours also held him in high regard. While he appeared to take his responsibilities very seriously, at the same time, he took time out of his busy schedule to comfort a small child. Perhaps she had been too harsh in her initial condemnation of him.

She felt the truck slowing down, and looked up in surprise to see that they were already coasting to a stop in front of the house. Tiffany, who had evidently been watching for them, ran from the house calling bright greetings. The cessation of motion awakened Ronnie, and she stretched against Susan. Then Burke lifted the small girl from the seat and, cuddling her against his shoulder, carried her towards the house. Slightly chilled by the removal of Ronnie's warm little body, Susan suffered a pang of loneliness as she watched the trio, Tiffany taking two steps to each one of Burke's while Ronnie sleepily detailed the day's adventures. Of course Burke was kind and gentle in his relations with Ronnie. It was only to be expected that his love for Tiffany would also encompass her daughter.

CHAPTER SIX

THE days of the Christmas countdown flew by. Elizabeth, somewhat confined because of her still weak leg, preferred to stay around the house, so it was Ronnie who was Susan's constant shadow, especially out of doors. Tiffany appeared to spend more and more time at her father's ranch, muttering vaguely about chores and responsibilities each time she left. The possibility of Tiffany actually making a decision seemed so remote that Susan privately wondered whether the Senator's ranch manager and hired help simply ignored her and went about their business. It did seem odd that Tiffany spent so much time away from Burke, but then Susan reasoned that perhaps the other woman was still trying to make up her mind. After all, even if she did love Burke, she had been living in New York City for some years now, and maybe she was reluctant to leave the big city for the radically different ranch life. Perhaps by spending so much time on her father's ranch, away from Burke's influence, she hoped to discover if she could be happy back in Colorado.

Burke appeared unbothered by Tiffany's frequent absences, so no doubt he understood her dilemma. Susan had caught a glimpse of them once in absorbed conversation, and it was readily apparent to her in the quick minute before Burke ushered Tiffany into his office that he was trying to talk the reluctant woman into something. Susan was troubled that he was taking advantage of the confidences she had let slip to force Tiffany into some type of commitment. Careful study of the two of them at mealtime, however, failed to give her any clue as to how Burke's courtship was progressing. Tiffany was a will o' the wisp, not to be pinned down by subtle questioning, and Susan was reluctant to ask outright if she had asked Burke to marry her.

Fortunately, there was too much to do on the ranch to brood over others' difficulties—new-born calves to see, baby kittens to play with, and of course, Elizabeth's wild birds to feed. If Burke was waiting patiently for Tiffany to make up her mind, he was seriously courting her daughter. Perhaps he felt if Tiffany saw how Ronnie adored him, she would marry him for the sake of her daughter. Susan soon grew to expect him to join her and Ronnie on their ranch excursions, discovering that he could be fun and entertaining company when he wished. Of course, he did get irritated when Susan insisted that she could climb the ladder into the hay loft, only to look supercilious when her foot slipped and he was forced to catch her. And he wasn't too happy when he found her carrying a bucket full of baby mice to release out in the fields away from the traps set in the barn. But he did agree with her that a kitten for Ronnie was a good idea, and she even sided with him once when, after they'd baked cookies one afternoon, having convinced a reluctant Vera to turn over her kitchen to them, he told a suddenly exhausted Ronnie that she had to help with cleaning up.

That was not to say that they began to agree on everything. To the contrary, they disagreed on most things. Susan couldn't stand the Country and

Western music that Burke insisted relaxed him. To
her, it was a lot of whining voices and twanging
guitars that irritated her nerves. Over dinner, Burke
baited her for drinking red wine while the others
were drinking white wine with their chicken.
Occasionally Susan wondered if Burke was taking
the opposite side of every issue just to be contrary.

At lunch one day, Elizabeth had feared that they
would come to blows over their differing positions on
farm aid. After that, Susan tried to keep politics out
of their mealtime conversation, realising that the
others suffered while the two of them battled. Susan
herself didn't mind the verbal skirmishes. Burke's
thought-out arguments kept her on her toes, and had
her devouring the daily newspapers for ammunition
to support her opinions.

Once, when he had arbitrarily made a decision for
the entire household and later informed them of it,
Susan had clicked her heels and saluted, letting him
know exactly what she thought of his dictatorial
ways. A clenched jaw was the only indication that
he'd seen her little display, but that night at dinner
he made a big show of asking everyone what he or
she wanted to do about Christmas Eve services. An
hour later, after a great deal of debate, indecision on
Tiffany's part and Elizabeth's asking Burke's opinion several times, it was at last determined to attend
Midnight Mass in Castle Rock. By this time, Susan,
who had missed a Christmas programme she had
wanted to watch on television because of the long
discussion, was doubly incensed when Burke murmured in her ear that he knew all along that was
what they would decide, and he'd already made all
the arrangements.

Christmas Day came and went, but the gay memories lingered on. Dawn had barely peeped over the low horizon before Ronnie was hustling everyone out of bed. Unwrapping the presents had been a happy, mad scramble with ribbon and paper flung to all corners of the room. Elizabeth was as delighted with the bird feeder as Ronnie had been with her myriad toys, and Burke had promptly installed the feeder on the deck outside Elizabeth's bedroom where the birds quickly discovered it.

Ronnie had, without question, received the most presents, but even Susan was remembered by everyone in the house party, and she was thankful that she had selected small gifts for everyone else. At Elizabeth's insistence, she had brought the unopened gifts from her relatives, and opened them on Christmas Day. Elizabeth had exclaimed over the exquisitely embroidered happi coat that Tom and Marie had sent from Japan, and Tiffany had declared herself green with envy when she had seen the chunk of malachite dangling from the gold chain, a gift from Mike and Linda.

From Burke, Susan had received a curious trio of paperback books. All dealt with young women who had moved to the West in the days it was being settled. Since all the heroines seemed singularly independent, and at the same time unprepared for the rigorous life they'd embarked on, there was no doubt in Susan's mind that Burke had selected the books with mischievous motives in mind. Pretending to be in ignorance of his intent, she had thanked him graciously for the books, and was gratified to see the devilish lights in his eyes give way to perplexity. Once she'd begun reading them, however, she had become so interested in the characters and so fascinated by the rich fabric of their lives that she'd forgiven Burke his joke at her expense. The truth was, the joke was on Burke, because the common theme of all the books was the inner strength of the women.

Susan's fingers moved nimbly over the ivory piano keys, and the light-hearted notes of a Broadway melody rippled through the living-room. Two days after Christmas, the lopsided tree hung even more drunkenly to one side, and fallen brown needles on the floor gave notice that it was time to it take down. Susan smiled reminiscently as she thought of the happy Christmas morning they had enjoyed, with Ronnie's joy and enthusiasm infecting everyone in the house.

The house was quiet now except for her singing softly in accompaniment to the sprightly melody. Tiffany's father was arriving at Denver airport early this evening, and Tiffany, along with Elizabeth and Ronnie, had gone eagerly to meet him; they were not due back until late at night. Susan had expected Burke to drive them, but a station wagon from the Senator's ranch, driven by his ranch manager, had come to pick the women up. In the flurry of their departure, Susan had met Neal Rutherford, the manager, and been left with an impression of quiet strength. Tiffany's indecisiveness, exaggerated by excitement, rendered her incapable of being ready on time, while Ronnie threw an uncharacteristic tantrum, refusing to leave without her favourite toy bear, which was temporarily mislaid. Even Elizabeth, normally the most placid of women, had dithered about until Burke had escaped to his office in disgust. But Mr Rutherford had dealt calmly with all the crises, real and imagined, and had soon bundled everyone into the car, winning Susan's life-long admiration.

Idly she wondered where Burke was now. He had gone out shortly after the others had left. Randy, she knew, had gone into town to meet with some of his college friends. Occasional sounds from the kitchen indicated that Vera was busy fixing dinner. Susan had already been bluntly informed by the housekeep-er that she worked better alone, so there was no point in volunteering to help her.

'Susan, I'm sorry to interrupt, but I just wanted to tell you about dinner.' Vera stood in the doorway, immaculately attired, as usual. 'Since there's just you and Burke for dinner tonight, Elizabeth told me to go home early. I put a casserole in the oven, and it should be ready in an hour or so. There's salad and dessert in the refrigerator. I'll do the dishes tomorrow.'

Thanking the older woman, Susan returned to her piano playing. She hadn't considered the fact that she and Burke would be sharing an intimate dinner for two. Hardly intimate in that huge dining-room, she reminded herself. Besides, Burke would most likely come in at the last minute, eat quickly, and immediately withdraw into his office. There wasn't anything for her to worry about.

She was still trying to convince herself of that, and at the same time wondering what she was worried about, some time later when she heard the front door open and close. Burke's firm steps sounded in the hall and then his office door slammed shut. After waiting a few minutes for him to reappear, Susan got up from the piano and walked to his office to deliver Vera's message about dinner and see when he wanted to eat. Pausing before the door, she unconsciously squared her shoulders. Why did she feel like Daniel bearding the lions in their den?

Taking a deep breath, she knocked on the door. The answering grunt was unintelligible, so she cautiously opened the door and peered inside. Burke was seated at his desk, his back to the door. Tufts of hair stood erect on his head as if he'd been wildly combing it with his fingers. Not deigning to turn and acknowledge her presence, he asked in an irritated voice, 'What do you want?'

'I just wondered when you wanted . . .' She broke off in confusion as Burke whirled around in his chair. The bleak look on his face startled her into speech. 'What's wrong?'

'Nothing.' He turned away, his stiff back an impenetrable barrier.

She tried again. 'When do you want to eat dinner?'

'I don't. Eat without me.'

Susan hovered in the doorway. Clearly Burke wanted to be alone. On the other hand, she hated to leave him when he was plainly troubled about something.

'Did you ever have a dog when you were growing up?' The question came unexpectedly.

'Not of my own,' she replied. 'We moved around too much. Sometimes the relatives we were staying with had dogs or cats.'

'I got a dog for Christmas when I was three. A beagle puppy. His name was Joey—Jumping Joey.'

Susan was pleased to hear the small note of amusement that had crept into Burke's grim voice.

'Jumping Joey?' She encouraged him to continue.

'We had a hand years ago, Old Charlie, everyone called him. Old Charlie's favourite expression was "Jumping Jehosaphat". Well, that puppy, he jumped all over me on Christmas Day. I had trouble saying Jehosaphat, so I dubbed the dog Jumping Joey. It's hard to explain the relationship between a kid and a dog, but Joey was my best friend. He followed me everywhere, slept with me. Once when I was rounding up cows, and my horse shied and threw me, Joey turned back a cantankerous old cow who thought she might like to grind me into dust.'

'He sounds like he was a very special dog. What happened to him?'

Burke stood up and crossed to the window, staring out into the dark. 'Died in his sleep when he was seventeen. Old age. Damn it!' He slammed his hand down on the window sill. 'That's how a dog should die—just quietly go to sleep. Not be shot to death!'

'Shot?' Susan was appalled at the implications of Burke's statement.

'Shot. How do you think it feels to have to go and tell a kid two days after Christmas that you shot his dog?'

The anguish in Burke's voice pierced Susan's heart, and suddenly he was not the arrogant male she verbally fenced with, but a small boy who had been somehow wounded. Instinctively she moved to stand behind him and gently touched his shoulders.

He grabbed her arms and held them tightly across his chest. 'Actually, José shot the dog because he had the rifle, but I told him to. *Damn*!'

Not knowing what to say, Susan hugged him tighter, her head resting against Burke's back, hoping he would understand that she was offering silent comfort.

'People never listen. The county sheriff, Ted Gaylord, warned Carter and the others just last week that their dogs were suspected of running in a pack. Of course they all denied that their good-natured pets could kill anything.'

'They actually killed?'

'First it was just running deer. Then, during the October snows, they caught one. The dogs can run on top if the snow is crusted, but the deer break through. They didn't even eat it. Then they started worrying cattle. Two weeks ago, a rancher down the road heard a commotion out in his yard and chased them away from his best mare and her new colt, right by the main house. He was the first to describe them to the sheriff. Then, a few days later, Neal Rutherford found one of their prize quarterhorses all tangled up in his paddock fence. The horse had to be put down. Dog prints were all over the yard.'

'How awful!' exclaimed Susan.

'It gets worse. A kid getting off the school bus late one afternoon was cornered on his way home. Luckily he was near a tall tree which he promptly climbed. His mom went looking for him a couple of hours later, and her car scared off the pack. The kid got a good look at the dogs and told the sheriff who asked around and figured out who the dogs probably belonged to. He went to visit all the owners, but of course by then all the animals were home and looking innocent as newborn pups. To a man, the owners denied that their animals had been out. Ted warned them that the dogs would likely be shot on sight, if allowed to run loose any more.'

'And you and José caught them today,' Susan guessed.

'They'd cornered a young heifer. We tried to scare them off, but that collie smelled blood, and he wasn't to be denied.'

'You can't fault yourself for doing what needed to be done. The dog turned bad.'

'It sure as hell isn't the dog's fault. There's no convincing some people that even if you live in the country, you can't let animals roam free. This particular pack all comes from those new housing developments. A couple of black labs, a mongrel or two, the Carters' collie, and even, for God's sake, a beagle. A bunch of loose dogs get together, and they revert to their ancestral behaviour—with a difference. Their ancestors hunted and killed for food. These dogs are well fed; they just hunt for the thrill, and after they kill something they head for home where they become once more the family pet. Even if they don't join a pack, the odds are if they run loose long enough, they'll end up getting hit by a car. And Carter had the nerve to stand there telling me how he loved that dog. Hell, if he'd loved the dog, he'd have taken better care of it. He even threatened to sue!'

'Surely he wouldn't stand a chance in court?'

'Of course not,' Burke said impatiently. 'The sheriff was with me, and he told him so. There are too many witnesses to testify to the dog's actions. He'll be lucky if the Senator doesn't sue him for loss of his stallion.'

Susan felt her way hesitantly. 'It must be a horrible feeling to have to kill a dog, as much as you loved yours.'

'Carter's got a kid about Ronnie's age. He told the

boy I'd murdered his dog. The kid started bawling and ran over and kicked me in the leg.'

'He should have kicked his father!' said Susan angrily.

Burke uttered a short laugh. 'I felt like it.' Some of the tenseness left his shoulders. 'Thanks for listening. I didn't mean to dump all my troubles on you.'

'You know us teachers, always listening to some kid's problems,' she joked, hoping to lighten the atmosphere.

Burke squeezed her hands before unwrapping them from his huge bulk. 'You said something about dinner. I'm not very hungry, but let me wash and I'll join you while you eat. Don't bother to set a place for me.'

Disregarding Burke's instructions, Susan put two plates on the table. Vera's casserole smelled heavenly, and with luck the aroma would stir Burke's appetite. Her aunt back in Nebraska always maintained that things looked better on a full stomach.

Burke arrived as Susan was setting the salad on the table. His eyebrows rose at the sight of the dishes at his place, but he said nothing. Dishing up her own dinner, she led the conversation to the books that he'd given her. She was surprised to learn that he had read all three, a discovery that certainly destroyed her theories as to why he'd given her the books. No one reading them could possibly be unaware of how positively the authors had portrayed women. Setting that discovery aside for later thought, she made a provocative remark about the role of women in history, and they were quickly engaged in a lively debate over women's contributions towards settling the western frontier. Although she refrained from comment, she was secretly pleased to see that Burke became so engrossed in their conversation that he absent-mindedly helped himself to the food.

He finished the last crumb of his cheesecake and put down his fork. 'Every schoolboy knows about the Pikes, the Fremonts, the Carsons, but I'll bet you can't name me one famous woman of the Old West.'

'Annie Oakley.'

'Big deal! A trick shooter in a Western show. That's not exactly saying she influenced history in any way.'

'Just because I can't name one, it doesn't mean they didn't exist. Men may be all you read about, but who do you think washed their socks or cooked their biscuits? Besides,' she challenged, 'men would have had a hard time populating the West without women, and in the final analysis, the abundance of people and towns are what tamed the West.'

Burke threw up his hands in surrender. 'You've got me there. If it wasn't for women, we never would have settled the West. Of course,' he added, '*they* couldn't populate the country alone, either.'

'I never said they could,' replied Susan virtuously. 'My only point is that that while it took equal effort, the women were just too darn busy to write about their exploits, so all we ever hear about are the men.' She stood up and began to gather their dirty dishes.

Burke picked up his own and followed her into the kitchen where he helped her clean up. When the dishwasher was finally industriously humming away, they returned to the living-room. To Susan's surprise, instead of shutting himself in his office, Burke suggested that they play cards.

'Since everyone else has abandoned you this

evening, it looks like it's up to me to uphold the family reputation for hospitality,' he said as he shuffled the deck.

Susan might have absolved him from any such responsibility, but she had no intention of allowing him to brood over the day's events. There was no doubt in her mind that what had upset Burke the most was the sight of the little boy who was grieving over the loss of his dog. His references to his own childhood pet told her that he had visualised himself in the little boy's place and was imagining all the pain that the other must be suffering.

They settled on gin rummy. Susan made sure that Burke kept his mind on the card game by insisting that they play for ten dollars a point. 'Purely imaginary,' she said at his look of horror.

Burke was good, but years of whiling away the hours on trains with her brothers had honed Susan's skills, and she was not the easy opponent that he had anticipated. After several hours of play, Susan sat back and chortled. 'I'll take some of your cows, your best horse, two gold mines and a lien on your house.'

'That's what I like: a good winner,' Burke said as he tallied up their final totals again in disbelief.

'Be glad I won. I'm a terrible loser,' Susan confided. Standing, she stretched to erase a crick in her neck. A yawn escaped before she could stop it.

'Winning all my money wear you out?' asked Burke drily.

'You know how it is. Wealth is such a burden,' said Susan airily. She looked at her watch. 'I thought Elizabeth would be back by now.'

'Knowing the Senator, he'll probably entertain them half the night with lurid tales of his Chinese adventures, some of them probably even true.'

Susan laughed. 'In that case, I think I'll say goodnight, and head up to bed.'

Burke caught her hand, preventing her from leaving. 'Thank you,' he said quietly.

Her pulse speeded up at the warm look in his eyes as he pulled her to him. 'Don't thank me,' she said breathlessly. 'I'm the one who won all the money.'

'You know what I mean,' he murmured as his head dipped towards hers. His lips felt cool and soft against hers. In the background, the records that Burke had put on earlier were still playing, a slow, sensuous beat that mocked her racing heart. The scent of his aftershave mingled with the aroma of the Christmas tree in the corner. Even with her eyes closed, sparkling lights danced in her head, and she felt giddy with inexplicable anticipation. A large hand on her lower spine ground her hips closer to Burke's male firmness, and the warmth from his large body enfolded her. When his mouth sought admittance, she eagerly welcomed him.

There was no coherent explanation for what she was doing, but she felt compelled to give Burke whatever he wanted. When a rough thumb trailed down the side of her neck and traced the neckline of her blouse, she trembled, but didn't pull away. When exploring fingers dipped lower, thrusting aside obstacles such as buttons, her only reaction was to turn slightly in Burke's arms, allowing him greater access in his quest. Wisps of lace were no barrier to determination, and Susan's breasts were soon swelling to fit Burke's soothing palms. His gentle manipulations quickly drew from her tremors of longing. She had no notion of passing time. There only existed the here and now, the desire to please Burke and the need to quench her own burning thirst.

Burke withdrew his lips from hers, and slowly pushed her away. The loss of heat from his warm body chilled her, and she looked at him in confusion. He tipped her head back, his hand firm beneath her chin while he gently stroked her bottom lip with his thumb. His skin tasted salty with a faint, clinging residue of soap. She dropped her eyes before the intense look in his, and in so doing, was at once aware of her blouse gaping open, disclosing rosy nipples hardened with desire. Swallowing a sob, she made haste to cover up. Burke's large hands caught hers and held them still. With slow, deliberate movements, he bent and bestowed a light kiss on each pink nub. When she made a move to pull away he dropped her hands at once, making no effort to stop her as she fled for the hall and the stairs to her bedroom sanctuary.

Safe in her room, his parting words echoed in her head. 'Sometimes I think you are too generous, Susan.'

She forced her wobbly legs to carry her to her bed where she collapsed in despair. How could she have kissed Burke like that, shedding all self-restraint? Tears welled up in eyes. She was a fool. There was no point in trying to kid herself that she had been trying to comfort him. When had she fallen in love with him? How could she have been so blind as not to recognise what was happening to her? The discontent, her jealousy of Tiffany's happiness, her own pain when Burke was hurting. She had tried to hide from herself what was happening, tried to convince herself that Burke was an arrogant, self-centred individual whom she despised, but the truth was, the more she was around him, the more she realised how many good qualities he had. There was no question but that he was arrogant, liked to have his own way, and disliked having someone, especially a woman, point out his errors. On the other hand, his agonising tonight over the day's events and his suffering for a child he didn't even know pointed out his sensitivity. The fact that everyone on the ranch held him in great esteem should have told her from the very beginning that there was more to Burke than she was giving him credit for. Maybe Burke was their boss, but you can't buy respect. And even as she'd admired his behaviour with Ronnie, she had discounted it as the act of a man in love with the child's mother.

The child's mother. Tiffany. Susan threw herself down on the bed and pounded on her pillow in frustration. How like her to look upon all men with disdain, and then when she did finally fall in love, to do so hopelessly with a man who loved another woman. She was too generous, Burke had said. When she would have given freely to him, he had pushed her away. His words were a kind reminder that he was not free and that it wasn't right that he accept her offering of love. Kindness. She didn't want kindness. She wanted his love.

Unrequited love. What a laugh. The independent woman who didn't need a man, loving and wanting a man who loved someone else. The tears streamed down her face, and she cuddled herself in her arms. Her breasts were still aching and tender with need. It was hopeless. Was it? Wasn't she a fighter? Hadn't she herself berated Tiffany for not being willing to fight for her man? The memory of Tiffany's face glowing with love settled over her like a heavy, woollen cloak, stifling the errant ray of spirit. Even supposing it were possible for her to win Burke from Tiffany, she couldn't do it. Tiffany needed Burke. And so did Ronnie. Susan could never be happy knowing that she had deprived Ronnie of the fatherly love that she so desperately sought.

Hours later she stared wide-eyed at the ceiling, her tears long ago dried up. Life had dealt her hard knocks before. She had coped then, and she would cope now. In a few more days she would be back home in her own apartment. Then she could forget about Burke, forget what had transpired this evening. Burke Gerard was not for her, and the sooner she faced that fact, the better for her.

She had no fears that what had happened would interfere with her friendship either with Elizabeth or Tiffany. By now she knew Burke well enough to know he was too honourable ever to kiss and tell. Even if the other two women did happen to find out, what did it matter to them? Susan was the loser. They were both getting what they wanted, she thought bitterly. Elizabeth was getting the daughter-in-law she doted on, and Tiffany was getting a second chance with the man she loved. For a second she hated the young widow. Tiffany had discarded Burke once, and now, it appeared all she had to do was crook her finger to win him back. It wasn't fair.

Fair. Life wasn't fair. How many times had one of her uncles told her that? Was it fair that Tiffany was beautiful, had an enchanting daughter and owned Burke's heart? Was it fair that she'd been devastated by the death of her husband at so young an age?

What was fair? She liked Tiffany; how could she begrudge the other woman her chance at happiness? Too many people in this world were suffering far more than Susan. Surely it wasn't too much to ask of her to hold her head high for the next few days. No one need ever know how badly she was weeping inside.

'All you have to do is get through the next few days,' she jeered softly to her twin in the mirror. 'Sure, easy for you to say.' Pausing in the midst of applying her make-up, Susan allowed her mind to wander back over the past several days. Some minor crisis had arisen in the Denver office, necessitating Burke's presence there. His absence had left her with ambivalent feelings. On the one hand, it was a relief not to be around him, having to pretend that she didn't care, but conversely, she longed to be in his presence, to gather memories and impressions to sustain her when she returned to Denver herself, and he was no longer in her world.

Life had been made somewhat easier by the removal of Tiffany and Ronnie to the Senator's ranch. Logically Susan refused to blame the other woman for her own inner pain, but emotionally, she resented the very fact of her existence. She missed the chatter of the small child, but she suspected that eventually she might even have come to be irritated by her, knowing that Ronnie was another reason that Burke belonged to Tiffany.

Fortunately Elizabeth was so full of the stories the Senator had regaled her with that she didn't seem to notice that Susan was struggling with unhappiness. And if Susan didn't respond when the older woman

chatted about Burke's and Tiffany's growing closeness, Elizabeth's own satisfaction more than made
up for any lack of enthusiasm on Susan's part. Randy
teased her, Vera went silently and efficiently about
her daily chores, and Susan silently counted the
hours until she could retreat to Denver. Her
apartment began to seem like a far-away sanctuary,
a sought-after haven where she could curl up and lick
her wounds. The healing process could never start
until she could get away from this house which
shrieked of Burke at every step and turn.

Tonight was her last big ordeal. Senator Payton
was giving an enormous New Year's Eve party,
ostensibly to celebrate his homecoming from China,
but, according to Elizabeth, actually to sponsor
Tiffany back into society after her bereavement.
Susan had tried to decline the invitation that Tiffany
had personally delivered to her, on the grounds that
she wouldn't know anyone there, but the other
woman had been insistent.

She grimaced at her image in the mirror. She
might be the loser in this triangle that no one else
even knew existed, but at least she was going out in
style. Black silk jersey pants accentuated her long
slender legs, gathering tightly about trim ankles.
Very little of the silk jersey had been wasted in
fashioning the camisole top. The thinnest of straps
held up loose-fitting triangles of fabric that silkily
kissed her nipples with each movement of her body.
She twisted sideways, checking her appearance in
the mirror. The rounded curve of a breast was plainly
visible. Nestled in the shadowy vee between her
breasts, the polished green malachite stone from
Mike was cool against her flushed skin. The memory

of Ronnie repeating Burke's remark about her being an old maid crossed her mind. No one would accuse her of that tonight. Crossing to the bed she sat down to strap on wickedly high-heeled sandals. Since she was going with the entire Gerard family, all noted for their height, for once she could play up her own instead of trying to disguise it.

A sharp knock scattered her thoughts. 'Susan? Are you dressed? May I come in?' Burke called from the other side of the connecting door.

She'd known he was back; she had been aware for the past hour that he was moving around in his room and the connecting bathroom. Even without the telling noise, she would have known he was around by the tingling of her skin, her feeling of being vitally alive. She hadn't seen him since the night they'd played cards, but the memory was still embarrassingly vivid. 'Come in,' she answered nervously.

'It's these darn cuff links of . . .' Burke walked into the room, only to stop abruptly and stare.

Pretending indifference to the stunned look on his face, she questioned, 'What about your cuff links?'

'I . . .' he cleared his throat, 'I can't get them fastened.' He made no move to approach her, however, but continued slowly to scan the length of her body.

'Well?' she demanded. 'Do you want help or not?' A flush of embarrassment crept up her neck at his frank, appreciative perusal.

'What? Oh, yes, the cuff links.' Walking over to where she stood in front of her dressing table, he extended one arm, the white cuff flapping.

Struggling to force the gold clasp through the double openings, Susan could feel the warmth emanating from Burke's body. Finishing one cuff, she looked up to find him gazing with interest at the large expanse of chest exposed by the daring top. His grey eyes brimmed with amusement. 'Give me your other arm,' she snapped.

Silently he obeyed. As she wrestled with the second link, she told herself she would not ask him what was so funny. The cuff fastened, she stepped away. 'There. It's done.' Refusing to meet his eyes, she turned away on the pretence of looking in the mirror to straighten her hair.

She looked, not at herself, but at his image that shared the glass. The black and white of his formal attire emphasised his massive shoulders and lean hips. He was still near enough that his sharp, tangy aftershave mingled with the mellow fragrance of her own perfume. She could hear others walking in the hall, but the two of them seemed cocooned in a silent world of their own. His mouth quirked up at the corners, and his laughing eyes met her disturbed ones in the mirror. She drew a shaky breath and concentrated on his black bow tie. 'You're laughing at me,' she accused in a voice mysteriously dry.

'I wasn't laughing at you,' he denied. He bent down and nuzzled her neck. 'That perfume you're wearing ought to be illegal. It's a deadly weapon!'

She jerked her head away from his electric touch. 'You're not laughing at my perfume,' she insisted.

'All right,' he conceded. 'I was laughing, but not at you. You look stunning, and you know it. It's just that almost as soon as I saw you, there flashed across my mind the picture of Mrs Dixon.' He stepped closer, using her mirror to adjust his tie.

'Mrs Dixon?' She held herself rigid, refusing to

melt into his warmth behind her.

'She used to teach at the country school where I went for several years. Mrs Dixon was about sixty years old, with grey hair that looked like little metal springs all over her head.' One hand flicked the hair curling against Susan's cheek. 'She had a fondness for pink nylon dresses. However, my most vivid memory of Mrs Dixon is that she always had a bra strap hanging down her arm, and was for ever reaching inside her dress and hauling it up.' Burke's fingers slid under one of the straps that held up Susan's top. 'Somehow I don't think lingerie is going to be a problem for you tonight.'

'No,' she agreed, trying to ignore his burning fingers as he toyed with the strap.

Abruptly his fingers stilled and then withdrew from her shoulder. 'Aren't you worried you'll get pneumonia?'

'I have a wrap.' She pointed to the heap of silk on her bed, black, with vivid hues of red, pink and purple shimmering in the glow of the bedroom light. 'My Christmas present from Tom and Marie.'

'One brother in Japan and the other somewhere else far away, I believe I heard you say on Christmas Day.'

'Germany,' she replied as she picked up the wrap.

He took it from her and draped it over her shoulders. 'That's tough, having your family spread out so much. You must miss them.' His eyes followed hers to the family photo she had placed on the make-up table. 'Those your brothers?'

'Yes, and their wives and children.' Miss them? Yes, she guessed she did. All these years she had fought their interference and ignored their well-meant advice. Now, when she needed their words of wisdom, they were out of touch. Some comedian's idea of justice.

'Hey, come on, smile! We're going to a party, not a wake!'

CHAPTER SEVEN

HOURS later, Susan had to admit it was quite a party. Burke had played the attentive host and introduced her to most of the other guests, but it seemed to her that Tiffany and her father had invited the entire population of Colorado. Thank goodness no one seemed to expect her to be able to remember names and match them with faces.

If, as Elizabeth had suggested, this party was Tiffany's re-introduction into society, it was a smashing success. Looking radiant in a bright red lace dress that swayed seductively with her every movement, Tiffany was inevitably the centre of a small group of men. Susan smiled. The tiny, raven-haired woman captivated everyone who came in contact with her. Seeing their husbands hanging on to Tiffany's every word might arouse jealous thoughts in the wives, but even they could not blame Tiffany for an unconscious gift that had no doubt been bestowed upon her in the cradle. No wonder Burke was smitten with her, and could forgive her anything, even jilting him.

That wasn't a thought that Susan cared to pursue, so she was thankful when Burke interrupted her musings to hand her a glass of wine. He said nothing, however, and she glanced up to see his gaze riveted on Tiffany where she now stood speaking to Neal Rutherford, her father's ranch manager. As if his gaze were a string pulling her, Tiffany looked up and smiled at Burke. A quiet word and a pat on the arm to the man beside her and she flitted across the room in their direction. Due to the surge of people at the door when they had arrived, Susan had had time only for a quick hello to Tiffany before Burke had urged her on into the house. Since then there had been little opportunity for them to talk.

There was an air of suppressed excitement about Tiffany. 'You look fabulous, Susan! I'm so glad you were able to come. This is a very special night for me, and I wanted you here to share it with me.' At Susan's obvious look of bewilderment, she gave a breathless laugh. 'You'll understand later,' she promised. 'And I owe it all to you. If you hadn't shown me that I had to stop acting like a kite in the wind, blown every which way with every gust ... your strength and independence gave me the courage to fight for what I wanted.' Turning and smiling tremulously at Burke, she added, 'As for you, dearest Burke,' before bestowing a light kiss on his cheek, 'I'll always love you.'

The room took a dizzying turn for Susan. Even though she'd known all along that Burke and Tiffany planned to resume their interrupted courtship, having the situation put into words gave her added pain. The final irony was that she was the one who had given Tiffany the fatal push. Before she could force herself to congratulate the two of them, there was a welcome interruption.

'What are you doing monopolising two of the prettiest gals in the room?' Howard Webb's booming voice preceded him as he greeted Burke. Wearing a stetson and cowboy boots with his tuxedo, the man once again failed to present the image of the staid banker. The lovely brunette tightly clasped in his arm greeted Burke and Tiffany warmly before turning to Susan.

'Susan, hard as it is to believe, this is Leslie Webb, Howard's wife,' Burke began.

'What do you mean, hard as it is to believe?' the big man blustered before Burke could introduce Susan.

'He means no woman in her right mind would be married to you,' Mrs Webb said, the teasing lights that danced in her eyes refuting her long-suffering tone of voice.

'Then it's lucky for me you weren't in your right mind when you met me, right, honey?' He squeezed her even tighter, if possible.

Mrs Webb smiled up at the huge man beside her. 'Lucky for both of us, I think,' she said softly.

The love in the glances exchanged by the two brought a lump to Susan's throat.

'If you two lovebirds can quit billing and cooing for a minute, I'd like to introduce Susan to Leslie,' said Burke.

Soft colour stealing over her face, Leslie Webb turned back to Susan. 'I'm sorry. I know who you are, of course. Elizabeth has told me all about how you helped her, and Howard told me he had met you the other day in town. It's lovely to meet you at last, Susan.'

With a wave of her hand, Tiffany had drifted away while the others were talking, and now stood deep in conversation with her father and Neal Rutherford.

Rocking back on his heels, Howard watched the trio. 'There's more to this than just a New Year's Eve party,' he mused shrewdly. 'I wonder what's up.' Glancing over at Burke, he asked, 'You know?'

Still struggling to compose the emotions exacerbated by Tiffany's blatant display of affection for Burke, Susan was happy the conversation had been directed away from her. She felt Burke shrug.

'I think your questions are about to be answered, Howard.'

Her interest caught by Burke's words, Susan watched Tiffany as the petite beauty stood whispering excitedly in her father's ear.

Holding up his hand for silence, the Senator cleared his throat and signalled for everyone's attention. 'First of all I want to welcome all our friends and neighbours for coming out tonight,' he said in his rasping voice. 'Tonight is a very happy occasion for me, and I'm pleased to have you all here to celebrate with me . . .' he paused, allowed his words to sink into an appreciative and eager audience, 'because tonight, we're celebrating not only the beginning of the new year, but the beginning of a new life for my daughter Tiffany and my granddaughter Ronnie. All right, all right,' he smiled down at Tiffany in response to an elbow in his side, 'Tiffany wants me to quit speech-making and get on with the announcement.' A few 'hear, hears' from his audience brought on a grin, but the Senator doggedly stared them down before clearing his throat portentously. An immediate hush fell throughout the room. 'It's my pleasure this evening to announce the upcoming marriage between my daughter and . . .' Here the Senator paused to flick a quick glance over to the side of the room where Burke stood with Susan. 'Between my daughter and my good friend, Neal Rutherford.'

A bomb couldn't have created a more dramatic silence. Susan had to bite her lips to prevent a nervous giggle from escaping at the astonished looks on the faces of those around her. No wonder Tiffany had been so nervous earlier! The few seconds of stunned silence might have been hours, and then Burke jolted the shocked crowd with his rousing applause. Quickly Susan joined in. The noise brought everyone else to their senses and the engaged couple was warmly applauded, with people surging towards Tiffany and her fiancé to personally add their congratulations. The red flush of embarrassment that had begun to crawl up Neal's face subsided in the wake of everyone's sincere wishes, and Tiffany gradually relaxed her defiant hold on his hand. The Senator beamed impartially and benevolently on the room at large.

In the confusion, Susan risked a look at Burke's face, but there was nothing there to give her any clue to his emotions. Following quickly on her first joyful feeling that Burke was now free was the sobering thought that he must be very hurt by Tiffany's actions. Even though he was putting on a good show of not caring and of being pleased for Tiffany, the fact remained that he had been expecting to marry her himself and now he had been jilted again. A tremendous feeling of anger against Tiffany for her heedless behaviour ripped through Susan. How could she put Burke through this experience once again? Almost at once the realisation of what Burke would have to endure was demonstrated by the Webbs.

Leslie pressed Burke's arm warmly. 'She never

was right for you, Burke.'

He smiled down at his well-meaning friend. 'I know that, Leslie. Don't worry about it.'

Howard gave a broad wink to Susan. 'I can't get it through Leslie's pretty little head that Burke's prospecting a whole different claim this time. The whole town's been set on the fact that Tiffany came back to marry Burke. Guess I'm the only one who knew different.'

Immediately the thought flashed through Susan's mind that here was a solution to Burke's problem. Instinctively she knew that he would hate all his friends and neighbours to pity him and gossip behind his back. Linking her arm in Burke's, she smiled coyly at Howard. 'I think you have an overactive imagination.' She hoped she wasn't being too subtle for the Webbs. She wanted them to believe that she and Burke had something going, while at the same time she realised that if Burke suspected that she was putting on an act because she felt sorry for him, he wouldn't be pleased.

Leaving the Webbs to cogitate over her careful non-denial, she edged Burke away. 'Let's go and congratulate Tiffany and Neal,' she urged. As they walked away, she forced a couple of coughs. 'I guess I've been talking too much. My throat certainly is dry.' She wanted to give Burke a little more time to recover from Tiffany's surprising announcement.

'What you need is some of that champagne that the Senator is doling out with such a generous hand.' An arm around her, he guided her towards the refreshment table.

Susan had no difficulty in playing the part in which she had cast herself. She thought back to the times she'd been in Burke's arms and simply pretended to herself that he had meant his kisses. After that, it seemed natural to touch him as frequently as possible, rub her cheek against his shoulder, and smile warmly into his eyes. If he was puzzled by her behaviour, he hid it well behind a façade of proud possessiveness, so convincing that Susan was in danger of forgetting that she was merely playing a role. Others in the room had no trouble interpreting their actions, and Susan was gratified to see that the initial surge of sympathy for Burke appeared to be swept aside by their curiosity about her.

Leslie Webb, coming up to her when Burke had been called away by friends to settle some argument, confirmed her success. 'I should have remembered that beneath Howard's country boy mask lies a very astute person,' she admitted.

'Meaning?' Susan remained non-committal.

'He's a very shrewd judge of people. I should have listened when he said Burke was interested in you.'

'Nonsense, we're just good friends.' Not for anything would Susan make a remark that might be quoted back to Burke with disastrous results.

Leslie frowned. 'I hope you're not playing games with Burke. That could be dangerous.'

'It's common sense she lacks, Leslie, not courage. Susan loves to flirt with danger, don't you, Susan?' Deep tones from behind Susan made her jump.

She turned to see Burke eyeing her speculatively. Several glasses of champagne made her reckless, and she reached up to caress his cheek with her hand. 'I must,' she answered his question. 'I love to flirt with you.'

Hooded eyes met her challenging ones before Burke grabbed her hand and tucked it in the crook of his arm. 'It's a shame your brothers didn't beat some sense into you when you were younger,' he said softly. To Leslie he added, 'I'm afraid I have to drag Susan away; Elizabeth has someone she wants her to meet.'

As Burke dragged her off, Susan called back over her shoulder, 'I'm counting on you to rescue me if Burke starts beating me, Leslie.'

Leslie's laughing reply was lost in the ringing of bells and tooting of horns as the clock struck midnight, and the party-goers raucously saluted the New Year. Burke manoeuvred Susan into a corner. His eyes searched her face for an eternal second and then his lips slowly descended. Susan's lips parted as if on command. As Burke's mouth found hers, she floated away on a timeless sea of effervescent waves and sparkling stars. The noise, the merry-makers, all faded away before the magic that Burke's lips were working on her. Sanity flooded back as she felt warm hands cradle her hips, and she broke loose from his arms.

He allowed her to step back only so far. 'Happy New Year, Miss Osborne.'

'Happy New Year, Mr Gerard,' she answered breathlessly. 'I thought you said Elizabeth wanted me to meet someone.'

'She did, but this seemed more important.' He dipped his head, and she was drawn to him as if to a magnet.

'One kiss to a customer,' a rasping voice said laughingly behind her.

Susan whirled around.

Senator Payton, Tiffany's father, stood there, a beaming Elizabeth at his side. 'Been wanting to meet you, young lady. I've heard Elizabeth brag on about you, and the last few days all Ronnie's done is talk about her good friend, Susan. It appears that you've been a mighty good influence on both my grand-daughter and daughter.'

As Susan stuttered a reply, she dared not glance at Burke. How soon would he start to put remarks together and come up with the conclusion that Susan was at least partly responsible for this evening's startling announcement? When he did, he would be furious. The fact that her intentions had been good would not spare her his anger. Interfering, busy-body—those were only two of the names he would call her again. He'd never believe that she had thought she was helping him.

Hiding her tumultuous thoughts, she managed to reply to Senator Payton. A born raconteur, he soon had her giggling helplessly at his stories. After listening to one improbable tale, she glanced up to Burke to share her amusement, only to flush hotly at the warm look in his eyes as he smiled down at her. He chuckled before reaching out one long arm and tucking her firmly against him. After that, Susan had no idea what Tiffany's father said. Her senses were totally occupied with Burke's presence, his scent, the warm, heavy feel of his hand resting on her hip, the realisation that she had only to turn her head to rub her cheek against his shoulder. The temptation to melt into his side was overwhelming. The shaking of his body alerted her that the Senator had finished another story, and she laughed dutifully.

Burke frowned down at her. 'Getting tired?' he asked softly.

Gratefully she grasped at the straw he offered her. 'A little.'

'Elizabeth, I think we're keeping Susan up past her bedtime. How about you?'

'It's been a very exciting evening, but I'm ready to call it a day. I'm too old to keep these late hours.'

'You'll never be too old,' said Senator Payton gallantly.

'Tiffany is busy now, but tell her I'll give her a call tomorrow. I'm so pleased for her, Ron. You don't mind?' Elizabeth asked anxiously.

'Nope, whatever my little girl wants is okay by me. She was kinda worried that I might not take to the idea of her and Neal, him being my manager and all, but heck, I know a man when I see him.' He laughed heartily. 'And so does Tiffany. She asked him, you know. He wasn't about to aspire to the boss's daughter. Tiffany told me that she had the gol-durnedest time getting him to agree to the marriage. He wasn't real wild about this shindig tonight, either, but I told him, out here we know how to judge a man, and it's not by the size of his bank account.'

'I'm sure that they'll be very happy,' said Elizabeth softly.

'Ya know, Tiffany said the funniest thing. She said Neal is the first man who treated her like a woman instead of a little girl.' His eyes grew suspiciously moist. 'She'll always be my little girl to me.'

Burke cleared his throat. 'Since we're standing by the door, why don't you two wait here while I go fetch our coats,' he said to Susan and Elizabeth.

They nodded in agreement and he strode away, the Senator at his side.

'It will probably take him an hour to return,' Elizabeth said in amusement. 'He'll be stopped a hundred times. We can only hope that he remembers what he's after.'

Susan absent-mindedly agreed. She was thinking over Senator Payton's words. All the time that she had thought Tiffany was talking about Burke, she'd been talking about Neal. All her worry about pride was based on Neal's being reluctant to marry Tiffany, who was not only rich in her own right, but also his boss's daughter. It had nothing to do with Burke's injured pride over being jilted.

'What a surprising evening this has been,' Elizabeth observed.

'It certainly has,' agreed Susan wholeheartedly. 'I didn't have a clue about Neal.'

'I suppose we should have had. It seemed strange that Tiffany was spending so much time at the ranch. I couldn't imagine that her father had delegated any of the responsibilities for it to her. I thought perhaps he had asked her to keep an eye on things as his way of trying to keep her mind occupied, but then that seemed foolish when I knew that he was hoping her stay at our place would resurrect her old relationship with Burke.'

'I know you were counting on that, too, Elizabeth. I'm sorry.'

'All I want is for both Burke and Tiffany to be happy,' said Elizabeth simply. 'If they found that happiness together, fine. But the fact that they found that happiness separately pleases me just as much. I can't tell you how happy I am, Susan, for you and Burke.'

'Oh no!' Susan gazed in horror at the older woman. She hadn't stopped to think, when she'd set out on her path to deceive Burke's friends and neighbours, that Elizabeth might gain the wrong impression also. 'Not Burke and me. I mean—that is—well, you know how we always fight,' she stuttered.

Elizabeth smiled serenely. 'That was my first clue. I've been suspicious for some time. Tonight simply confirmed it. I'm so pleased. When I first met you, I thought how right you were for Burke, but of course then I thought he had his mind set on Tiffany. I should have realised his heart was waiting for you to come along.'

'I'm sorry, Elizabeth. What you think simply isn't true.'

'But tonight? A blind person could tell that you're madly in love with Burke,' Elizabeth said in bewilderment.

Susan bit her lip. This wasn't going to be easy. 'I'll try to explain. I . . . I know how people expected that Tiffany had come home to marry Burke. The thought of everyone feeling sorry for Burke was just more than I could bear. I thought if they thought that Burke and I—well, you see, don't you?'

'I see more than you think I do,' Elizabeth said gently. 'Didn't it occur to you to wonder about Burke's motivation in following your lead?'

'Even if he doesn't admit it to himself, I'm sure that Burke's ego appreciates having me hang all over him and take away some of the speculation about whether he is hurt over Tiffany's second defection.'

'And what about the speculation when you leave, and everyone realises that your performance here this evening was nothing more than that? Don't you think that everyone will feel even sorrier for Burke that he was so devastated by Tiffany's actions that he needed you to pretend to be in love with him? Do you really think that his male ego is so fragile that it could be shattered by Tiffany's engagement to another man? I'm not sure your course of action here this evening was very wise.'

'You mean it was pretty stupid,' said Susan miserably. 'I just didn't think it through. Maybe after I leave you can tell everyone that I had a mad crush on Burke, and he was just being kind to me. It doesn't matter what people here think about me.'

'I'm sure it will all work out,' Elizabeth said kindly.

A heavy hand fell on Susan's shoulder, and she turned to look up into Burke's hooded eyes. 'Here's your coat. Sorry it took me so long. Senator Payton wanted me to meet someone.'

A slight tremor of fear ran through Susan. Had Burke overheard her and Elizabeth's conversation? Suddenly she was overwhelmed by the stupidity of her actions. Why had she been so precipitate? Burke was more than capable of taking care of himself; he didn't need her to shield behind. Elizabeth's gentle recriminations would be like praise compared to Burke's fury once he put two and two together and realised that she'd been trying to protect him this evening. She risked a glance in his direction. He was helping Elizabeth on with her wrap and smiling at something she said. Susan breathed easier. He hadn't heard them talking.

She wasn't so sure when he helped her into the large sedan. All three of them were riding in the front seat, as Randy had stayed behind at the party, and somehow Susan ended up tucked between Burke and Elizabeth. The conversation was general and filled with pleasantries about the party, but Susan could feel the tension radiating from Burke's thigh where it rode pressed against hers. Once, the centrifugal force from going around a curve pushed her against Burke's shoulder, and he stiffened at the contact. The long ride seemed endless, and it was with a sigh of relief that she spotted the ranch lights coming into view. She felt Burke's glance at her sigh, but he said nothing.

He stopped the car in front of the house to allow Elizabeth and Susan out. As he helped Susan from the car, his hand squeezed painfully tight on her arm. Once inside, Elizabeth was inclined to talk over the party, but Susan pleaded fatigue and fled to her room. She had no intention of being around when Burke returned from garaging the car.

Safe in her room, she relaxed. The past half hour she'd felt like a high-wire artist who couldn't see if her safety net were in place. Tossing her bag on the bed, she reminded herself that tomorrow the ordeal would be all over. She'd be returning to Denver, and school started the next day. That should take her mind off Burke. The children would be so eager to share their holiday adventures that she wouldn't have a moment to herself. That suited Susan just fine; she wouldn't have time to wonder if, now that Tiffany was going to marry someone else, Burke might look her way. She was too proud to take another woman's leavings. Wasn't she?

She never had a chance to answer her own question. Glimpsing movement out of the corner of her eye, she turned quickly to see Burke leaning with indolent ease against the doorjamb. The fierce look on his face belied the casual pose. Leslie's words about danger flooded back into her mind, and she could feel her knees start to quiver.

'What . . . do you . . . want?' she stammered.

'Surely you were expecting me?'

'Of course I wasn't expecting you. Why should I be?'

'It's the only logical conclusion to your behaviour tonight.'

'My . . . my . . . behaviour?' she parried.

Burke shook his head in mock disappointment. 'For a teacher, you certainly are slow to grasp a concept! And here I thought you'd be eager to discuss the fascinating subject of our relationship.'

'Relationship?'

'Must you parrot my every word? I'm referring, of course, to our . . . what would you call it, anyway? I'm curious. Are we having a love affair?' The savage glint in his eyes warned her.

'You're angry.'

'Whatever gave you that idea? A man would have to be extremely foolish to be angry just because a beautiful woman goes around telling people that she pities him.'

Angry sarcasm coated his words, and she edged away, uncomfortably aware of the leashed strength beneath his polished veneer. At her cowardly retreat, Burke impatiently ripped off his bow tie and moved closer. Like a tiger stalking his prey, she thought wildly.

'I'm . . , I'm sorry if . . . if my behaviour didn't . . . didn't meet with your approval this evening,' she began stiffly.

'You know damn well it didn't, and what's more, you knew it wouldn't. I neither want nor need your pity.' Moving swiftly to her side he grabbed her upper arms with hard hands, and hauled her close to his chest. 'Save it for old ladies, widows and ugly trees,' he snarled before thrusting her away from him as if the merest contact with her were distasteful to him.

Her arms smarting from his cruel grip, she backed away from him on trembling legs until she was brought up short by the side of the bed. Reaching out, she clutched the bed frame to support herself. 'I wasn't feeling sorry for you,' she insisted, but even to her own ears, the words carried little conviction.

'No? Then what was that cute conversation with Elizabeth all about?'

'You did overhear us,' she said weakly.

'Lucky for you,' he snarled. 'With the come-on you were giving me all night, how were you going to make sure that I didn't accept your warm invitation to join you in your bed?'

'It . . . I never . . . that is, I didn't think . . .'

'Damn right you didn't think. When have you ever?'

'I'm sorry,' she whispered.

Burke leaned back against the wall, arms folded in front of him, his anger not so easily placated by simple words. He was hurt and needed to hurt back.

Unease rippled through her. There was no doubt at all in Susan's mind whom Burke had selected to exorcise his pain on. Well, she wouldn't let him intimidate her. Giving notice that their discussion was over, she faked a huge yawn. 'I'm tired. Perhaps we could discuss this in the morning when you're less upset.'

Even to her own ears, the words sounded patronising, and it should have come as no surprise that her comment snapped the control that Burke had on his temper. A swift arm snaked out and jerked her up against his steel chest. Struggling to break free availed her not at all. Vaguely aware of his shirt studs digging into her chest, she beat on his shoulders with clenched fists until he captured her hands and forced them behind her back, one huge hand of his imprisoning them there. Leaning back to evade his punishing mouth only served to bring her hips in closer contact with his hard, muscled thighs. Catching her head in his remaining hand, he stilled her frantic movements.

Susan closed her eyes, dreading his harsh assault on her lips. Both were breathing heavily after the energetic tussle, and she could feel his harsh, panting breaths on her face. The smell of wine, combined with the sensual scent of his aftershave, whirled about her nostrils. In the background the ticking of a clock kept time with the thundering of her heart. Now that he had her in his power, Burke seemed content to toy with her. Aeons passed while he failed to follow up his advantage, and at last, Susan cautiously peered up at him from beneath lowered lashes. Hooded eyes and a brooding expression on his face did little to reassure her. Burke meant to make her pay the price for daring to pity him. Between her and Tiffany, they had dented his manhood. He intended to use Susan to heal himself.

The fear engendered by that thought gave her strength, and she renewed her struggles. Almost contemptuously Burke halted her puny efforts.

'Do you still feel sorry for me?' he asked remorselessly.

'No, I don't. I didn't!' she cried.

Burke raised a eyebrow in exaggerated disbelief. 'No? Then it must be the other.'

'Other?'

'A man would have to be a fool to turn down the obvious invitations that you were directing my way all evening. Even my worst enemy never called me a fool.'

'No!' Susan cried. Their silent struggle was intense, but definitely unequal. With contemptuous ease Burke controlled her, forced her head still to receive his kiss. More an assault than a caress, had it been possible Susan would have cried out when he brutally forced open her mouth and thrust an invading tongue into the soft depths. Fear of his intentions mingled with the strong tremors of desire that his hard body was arousing against her will. But no matter how much she loved Burke, she couldn't let him take her like this. Even one-sided, her love for him was too sweet to allow him to destroy it in one night of anger. The thought lent fuel to her efforts to escape him, and at last managing to free one hand, she swung wildly at him, finding his cheekbone with a resounding smack.

Burke was instantly still, and she quivered with fear at the thought of his retaliation. Fierce fingers dug into her shoulders as he held her away from him, studying her face. Flinging back her head for courage, she faced him defiantly, only to be betrayed by a lone tear which slipped down her cheek.

Burke uttered a short oath before gently licking away the tear and pressing her head down to rest against his shoulder. 'It's okay, Susan. I won't hurt you.' The room was quiet as he held her close against him.

A feeling of utter contentment pervaded Susan's limbs and, catlike, she rubbed her cheek against the smooth lapel of Burke's tuxedo. When he freed her arms, it seemed only natural that they found their way up around his neck. Rough thumbs massaged her shoulders before sliding the silky kimono down her arms. With her heightened senses, she could trace its slithery path down her back, over her hips and past her legs to the floor. The whispery sound teased nerve endings already aflame. Burke traced her hairline with feathery kisses before working his way around to nibble on her sensitive ear lobes. When he nudged her mouth into position to receive his kisses, this time she was eager to comply. One thin strap was slipped off her shoulder, and then the other. He brushed one large hand down her side and rested it on her hip, pulling her in tight against him. His thumb gently rubbed her skin just above the waistband of her trousers.

This time there was no thought of stopping him. She wanted him as much as he wanted her. What did it matter what his reasons were? She loved him, and in loving him, needed to heal his wounds; if she could do so by giving him her body, then it was right for her that she do so. Besides, just this once, she wanted to share with Burke the special closeness that comes only when a man and a woman give entirely of themselves. If she never saw Burke again, she would always have the memory of their lovemaking to keep within her.

'I thought we came home because I was tired,' she said, secure in the knowledge that he would know she was teasing him.

'Then you should be in bed,' he counselled, a warm hand searching beneath the silky fabric until it successfully located the sensitive tip of one breast.

She could feel the champagne bubbling through her veins. 'I planned to go to bed and sleep,' she murmured.

'You know what they say about the best-laid plans.' His hands were busy, and her camisole top dropped to the floor exposing her breasts to his view. Warm delicious sensations flowed down to her stomach, only to turn hot and wanting as Burke covered one of her breasts with his lips and slowly teased the hardening nipple. She arched her body, pressing closer to his demanding lips, and moaned as intense pleasure rippled through her body.

Burke leisurely licked his way upward, his tongue rasping against the nerve endings of Susan's skin. She shivered with anticipation as he guided her to her bed. Laying her gently down on her back, he unstrapped her sandals, and then removed the last of her clothing, until all she was wearing was the thin gold chain with the malachite pendant cradled between her breasts. Still dressed, minus only his tie, Burke stood beside the bed, his hungry eyes stirring delicious simmering sensations in Susan as he removed his shirt studs. From some deep womanly preserve that she never knew existed within her, there came the knowledge that her naked body pleased him, and she stretched sensuously to tantalise and torment him. A flame erupted in the smouldering grey eyes, and the small victory gave her a sense of power. She reached out with her hand to urge him on. Recognising her need, he smiled lazily, but he was not to be hurried. He slowly began to undress while at the same time admiring her body, his gaze so warm and possessive that Susan could almost feel its touch burning a trail up her body.

Suddenly Burke's eyes narrowed, there was a hint of disbelief, and then his face went stiff and totally empty of any emotion. 'I'm sorry. I'm afraid I allowed myself to get carried away.' Anger coated the cold words, and Susan flinched as he leaned over her, his fury a visible force. A muscle clenched in his jaw at her sudden movement, but he only shook loose a blanket from beneath her and threw it over her naked body. He turned to walk away.

'Burke, wait! I don't understand!' she sat up in the bed, the covers falling heedlessly to her lap.

Turning to reply, Burke immediately noticed Susan's naked breasts, and such a look of mingled pain and contempt crossed his face that she hastily slid beneath the blanket, shame flushing her skin.

'There's nothing to understand,' he said harshly. 'You said you were tired, go to sleep.'

'But I . . .,'

'Damn it, Susan, just drop it!' he exploded, his nostrils distended in anger. 'I understand you're leaving tomorrow.' He had himself under control now. 'I won't be seeing you in the morning, so I'll say goodbye now.' His face twisted into a sneer. 'It's been real educational, teacher.' He snapped off the light switch, and then slammed the door behind him.

Susan knew she should get up to remove her make-

up and hang up her clothes, but she was so
benumbed by Burke's hurtful words that a fire alarm
couldn't have moved her. What in the world had
happened? One minute Burke had been pleased by
her body—he *had* been. She couldn't have been
mistaken about that. The next minute, it was as if he
hated her. Curled into a miserable little ball in an
unsuccessful effort to warm her body, she couldn't
stop the tears that flowed down her cheeks.

More potent than any wine, Burke's lovemaking
had drugged her inhibitions while she had become
drunk on the taste, the smell and the feel of his body.
He had teased and tantalised her until she had
erupted in an explosive shower of shimmering
bubbles and shooting stars. Her willing response
hadn't shamed her until Burke had rejected her so
cruelly. Was he punishing her because it was really
Tiffany he wanted? Was his rejection revenge for her
daring to feel sorry for him? She would never feel
sorry for him again. How could he do something like
that to her? Even now her body ached for the
fulfilment that only he could offer her.

True to his word, Burke was not present when
Susan finally appeared at breakfast the next morning. Her eyes were red-rimmed and her voice husky
from crying most of the night, but Elizabeth
appeared to accept her explanation that she was
coming down with a cold virus. Whether Elizabeth
sensed her mood, or whether Burke had had a few
words with his mother, Susan never knew, but the
older woman said little over the breakfast table, and
the subject of the party the evening before was not
broached.

Her packing quickly accomplished, Susan stumbled through her goodbyes. Words stuck in her throat, and tears threatened, so, giving Elizabeth a quick hug, she climbed in her car and drove off, Elizabeth's strong sympathy a tangible presence beside her. Refusing to look around to see if she could catch a last glimpse of Burke, she stoically ignored landmarks that might conjure up memories of happier days. She would not look at the barn where Burke's strong arms had stopped her tumble, she chose not to see the snowman wearing Burke's old cowboy hat, and she had absolutely no nostalgic interest in the dried-up Christmas tree leaning against the fence. A boulder was her downfall. The sight of the rock where she and Burke had met so abruptly proved too much for her self-control. She cried most of the way back to Denver.

CHAPTER EIGHT

SUSAN slumped down in her seat. Even the golden daffodils along the pavement and the pale pink, flower-laden crabapple tree across the street could not penetrate the wall of tiredness and inertia that pervaded her body. The last day of school before a vacation was always exhausting, with active children doubly excited by the dual pleasures of a week's vacation and a party. True, the mothers who had come to help with the Easter party had been a great help in channelling excited energies into vigorous games, but still she felt absolutely drained. Today, questions that usually delighted her with their proof of inquisitive minds had only served to irritate her. More than once she had snapped at a child who had only been demonstrating initiative. Was she suffering teacher burn-out already?

Even as she asked the question, she knew the answer. Her problem lay not in her teaching, but in her private life. She didn't know why she had hoped to hear from Burke, but the weeks had passed without any sign that he had even remembered her existence. Elizabeth's letters continued with flattering regularity, filled with friendly gossip about the ranch and neighbours. She had written all the details of Tiffany's wedding, which had taken place only last week. Susan had been invited, and after long deliberation, had sent back a letter with her regrets.

Fighting the temptation to see Burke again, she told herself that such an encounter could only prove embarrassing for them both. Besides, hadn't Elizabeth written that Burke was an absolute bear these days, and that everyone was walking gingerly in an effort to stay out of range of his uncertain temper? The last thing she needed was for Burke to take out his anger on her again.

A passing neighbour, staring at her curiously, brought her out of her reverie. She'd better stop sitting in the car and take in the groceries. Ordinarily she would have been home several hours ago, but there had been a small gathering after school in the teachers' lounge, and then a very necessary trip to the grocery store was indicated. No wonder she was exhausted. She wanted nothing more than a hot bath and dinner. Perhaps . . .

'Where have you been?' The car door was savagely jerked open. An irate Burke Gerard stood beside it.

Her head leaning over the back seat as she'd gathered up parcels, Susan had failed to see his approach, and now she could only stare in disbelief. 'Burke!' Was that hoarse whisper hers? Awkwardly she climbed from the car, books and packages clutched precariously in her grip.

'Here, give me those.' Impatiently Burke grabbed those closest to disaster and slammed the car door shut behind her. A compelling hand in the small of her back propelled her irresistibly to the entrance of her apartment building. Burke's speedy ascent up the stairs left Susan too breathless to ask what he was doing there. At her door, she fumbled with the keys, her nerveless fingers failing to co-operate with a brain that was numb with the shock of Burke's sudden appearance. His looming presence did nothing to help the situation.

At last she managed to unlock and open the door. Before she could invite him in, Burke shoved in behind her and slammed the door shut with his hip. Had her apartment always seemed this small, this stuffy? Or was it Burke's being here, his rampant masculinity somehow threatening the sanctity of her refuge?

'Tiffany was upset you didn't come to her wedding,' he said, his scowling face accusing her.

'I . . . I was busy.'

'No, you weren't. You didn't come because of me.'

'If that isn't just like you! You are the most overbearing, arrogant male I've ever encountered! It may surprise you to know that I don't plan my life around your existence.'

Stormy grey eyes darkened. 'I don't believe that you could possibly be so busy that you couldn't take a couple of hours to . . .'

He never finished the sentence, because at that moment Susan's bedroom door opened, and Burke was staring in shock at the sleepy, unshaven man who emerged, obviously and inadequately garbed in Susan's old terry cloth robe.

'Gosh, I didn't mean to sleep all day. You should have awakened me before you left this morning, Susie.' The man stretched, and yawned. He was still half asleep, or he would have felt the electricity in the air generated by his appearance.

Burke dropped the packages he was still holding

on to the nearby dining-room table. Ignoring the ominous rip of paper, he turned furiously to Susan. 'Never mind. I think I can answer the question myself. Always a pleasure to run into you, Miss Osborne.'

The cold, biting words tore into Susan, and she could only stand mute, in stunned disbelief as Burke turned on his heel and slammed out of the door. The crash reverberated through the small apartment.

Mike looked at her in astonishment. 'Who in the world was that?'

A lone tomato rolled out of the torn sack and smashed on to the floor at Susan's feet. Looking down at the red pulpy mess decorating her white shoe, she burst into tears.

Mike swiftly crossed the floor between them and drew her into his arms. 'Want to tell your big brother all about it?'

'There's nothing to tell,' she sniffed.

'Well, you could start with who just slammed out of here.'

'Burke Gerard.'

'Gerard,' he mused. 'Where have I heard that name before?'

'He's one of Elizabeth's sons. You remember I told you about meeting Elizabeth Gerard.'

'Oh yes, the lady in the car park.' He frowned. 'I don't remember you ever writing about this Burke character, however.'

'Why would I? I hate him!' she wailed.

Mike hadn't been Susan's brother for twenty-four years without learning something, and he recognised that now was a good time to change the subject.

'Why don't I take a shower while you clean up this mess and put away the groceries, and I'll take you out to eat.'

Managing a tremulous smile, Susan agreed tearfully. And by the time she had finished and the shower had been turned off, she had almost convinced herself that she didn't care what Burke Gerard thought. So what if he had obviously jumped to the conclusion that her brother was somebody else. It served him right. She was still trying to decide how it served him right, when Mike came out from the bedroom, this time clean-shaven and respectably clad in slacks, a sports coat slung over her arm.

They were debating over where to eat when the doorbell pealed. To Susan's dismay, when she opened the door, Burke was standing there. At her instinctive move to slam the door in his face, he thrust her aside and stepped into the room, his hand outstretched in the direction of Mike. 'I have to apologise for my behaviour earlier. I left in such a hurry that I didn't give Susan a chance to introduce us. I'm Burke Gerard, and you must be one of Susan's brothers.' Burke glared at Susan over Mike's head.

Livid with anger, she glared right back. How dared he act like it was her fault he'd jumped to some nasty conclusion? She wondered how far he had gone before he'd recognised Mike from the picture that had stood on her dressing-table at the ranch. Not that she cared. Her chin rose a notch. 'I'm afraid we were just leaving,' she said, looking meaningfully at the door.

Both men refused to take her hint. After one

thoughtful glance at Susan, Mike had come forward and shaken Burke's hand, measuring him in the way that years of experience had accustomed Susan to. Just so had he measured every boy who had ever carried Susan's books home from school. She would quickly disabuse her brother of any notion that Burke was in any way a suitor for her hand. 'Mike,' she tugged at his arm, 'we were just going out, remember?'

'Sure, sure. Perhaps you'd like to join us for dinner, Mr Gerard?' he invited, ignoring the gathering storm clouds on Susan's face.

'He's already busy.' The firm chin challenged Burke to disregard her wishes.

He grinned at her, a savage, twisted grin that promised retribution. 'Thanks. I'd love to join you.'

'If he goes, I stay home,' Susan threatened childishly.

Mike shrugged. 'Okay.' Thrusting long arms into his tweed sports coat, he turned to Burke. 'You'll have to suggest the place. I'm afraid I'm not too familiar with Denver.'

'My pleasure,' Burke assented, amusement rippling across his face as he followed Mike from the apartment. Even through the closed door, Susan could hear the admiration in his next words, 'My God, is that how you handle her?'

Picking up the object nearest to her, Susan flung it against the door. Unfortunately it was another tomato, and she watched in horror as a sticky orange mess oozed down the door to lie in a messy puddle on the floor. 'Damn you both!' she cried. What right did Burke have to burst in here and ruin her evening? As for Mike, he was her brother. He was supposed to be on *her* side!

As the minutes ticked off and they didn't return, it occurred to Susan that they really intended to eat without her. Not that she wanted to go and eat or anything else with Burke Gerard, but she couldn't believe that her own brother could behave in such a callous manner. Tears flowed freely as she sopped up the mess on the floor. Wrinkling her nose at the acidic tomato odour that overpowered the room, she decided that a shower might at least remove the sticky residue from her hands and legs. Dark thoughts of both Mike and Burke kept her company as the warm water sluiced over her body, and if hot tears mingled with the water from the shower, who was to know?

It wasn't until she had stepped out and was towelling her hair that the questions began to nag at her. Why was Burke here? Why had he come to her place? He had indicated that he had been waiting for some time for her to come home. What did he want? Had Elizabeth sent him? Was there something wrong? Blast her unruly tongue that had sent him on his way before she'd even discovered what he wanted. Nibbling on the corner of her towel, she contemplated calling Elizabeth. Maybe she needed something. No, it would prove too embarrassing to have to explain why she didn't know what Burke had wanted. Maybe Burke would tell Mike. Of course, it would be just like Mike to tease her and refuse to tell what he knew. Brothers. Men! What had she ever done to be so tormented by them? Well, she'd make darn sure that Mike was heartily sorry for walking

out on her the way he had; how could the two of them
go off and leave her like that? Didn't they like her?
Tears started anew.

Totally awash in self-pity, she barely heard the
doorbell. Her first thought was to ignore it, but then
curiosity got the better of her. Slipping into the same
terry robe that Mike had donned earlier, she
wrapped a towel turban-style about her hair, hastily
wiping away any traces of tears. The doorbell pealed
again impatiently. Padding to the door on bare feet,
she halted, one hand on the lock. 'Who is it?'

'Burke.'

'Go away!'

'I want to talk to you.'

'I don't want to talk to you,' Susan snapped.

'I'm going to stand out here until you let me in.'

'Fine. Just stand there all night. See if I care.'

There was a small period of silence, and then she
could hear Burke speaking to someone in the hall.
'Hello. No, I'm not looking for anyone. I'm waiting
to talk to Miss Osborne, but she won't let me in. She's
angry with me because I took off all her clothes and
then didn't make love to her.'

Susan's eyes widened in horror at Burke's outrageous remarks. Frantically she unlocked the door
and reached out to pull him into the apartment.
Prepared to face the snickering face of one of her
neighbours, she was bewildered to see only Burke,
his six-foot-plus length leaning lazily against the
wall, the casual stance belied by the intensity of the
gaze he directed at her face. 'Who . . . who were . . .
you talking to?' she stammered, all pretence at poise
fleeing before the hungry look in his eyes.

'I knew that would get you out here,' he said, pushing her back into her apartment. 'I wasn't talking to anyone. I just didn't feel like standing out in the hall all night, and I know you're stubborn enough to make me.'

Shrugging out of his grasp, Susan walked over to a nearby window and pretended great interest in the passing traffic on the street below. Her towel threatened to slip from her head, and she removed it, aimlessly rubbing the dripping tendrils of hair that clung to her freshly-scrubbed face. Perhaps if she refused to acknowledge Burke's presence he would politely leave. A sudden tingling at the base of her spine told her that he had silently crossed the room and stood directly behind her. She could feel the heat from his body reaching out to her. 'What do you want?' she blurted out.

'You.'

Her stomach gave a tremendous flip-flop at his bald answer. She waited for the riot to subside before she answered. 'Sorry. Opportunity only knocks once.' The flippant reply was meant to disguise the hurt that seared through her body at his insolent answer. How dared he insult her so? Even as her anger flared, her body ached treacherously at the memory of Burke's arms.

'I hope that's not true,' he said gravely. 'I left your brother at the corner bar making wedding plans. As it was, I had all I could do to convince him that you would prefer to call his wife and your other brother with the news yourself.'

The brazenness of his reply left Susan speechless. She could only turn and stare at him. Enigmatic grey eyes steadily returned her appraisal. 'But I'm not getting married,' she blurted out. She thought the merest wraith of anxiety flashed across Burke's face, but it was gone before she could be sure.

Burke shrugged. 'I'm willing to just live together, if that's what you want, but I do think that explaining it to Elizabeth might be a little difficult, and I shudder to think what those two brothers of yours might do if they thought I was refusing to do the honourable thing.'

His mocking words inflamed nerves already on edge. Eyes shooting angry sparks, she turned away from him, clenching her robe with white-knuckled fists. 'Get out!'

Behind her there was silence, and then heavy footsteps headed towards the apartment door. She strained to hear the door open, her entire body filled with a terrible pain and loneliness that she knew would only intensify with the closing of the door. A loud slam made her jump, and started afresh the tears that had been lurking beneath lowered lashes.

A series of hard, biting oaths came from across the room, and she whirled around in surprise. Burke stood there, fiercely glaring at her, arms jammed in his trouser pockets. At the sight of the tears rolling down her face, his face softened. Swiftly he crossed the room and enfolded her into his arms. His rapid passage from anger to compassion only bewildered Susan more, and she buried her head in his shoulder, crying uncontrollably.

When at last the storm subsided, Burke was sitting on the sofa, and she was draped across his lap. Blowing loudly into the large handkerchief that he'd handed her, she ventured a peep from beneath tear-drenched lashes. Expecting to see his face blanketed with scorn, she was confused at the rueful look he gave her. She struggled to get up, but his arms were iron bands holding her in place. Refusing to meet his eyes which seemed to, but couldn't possibly, be brimming with tenderness, she concentrated on his neck where brown curls kissed his shirt collar. 'I'll leave just as soon as you tell me you don't want to marry me,' he said quietly.

'You don't want to marry me.' Stubbornly she resisted looking at him.

'I do.'

The simple words took her breath away. Slowly she looked up at him. The disturbing light in his eyes sent a thrill of hope throughout her body. 'What . . . about . . . Tiffany?' she whispered brokenly. 'I won't . . . won't be a substitute.'

Burke laughed, a low rumbling sound that vibrated his chest and sent corresponding tremors through Susan's body. 'Tiffany Tallerton—no, Tiffany Rutherford now—is, and always shall be, one of my favourite people. I love her.' Strong arms tightened at Susan's convulsive start at his admission. 'I love her like a sister,' he added firmly.

'But . . . but the engagement—her visit here,' Susan stuttered, trying to push away the deliriously happy hope that persisted in edging into her mind.

Burke sighed, shifting her to a more comfortable spot on his lap. 'I can see that you are going to demand the whole story. Never mind that it makes me look like a fool.' She nodded at his questioning look. She couldn't commit herself until she knew for sure where Burke stood. She refused to be Tiffany's surrogate.

'I've known Tiffany all my life. I never thought much about it. She was just always there. I took her to dances, and she cheered me on at all my ballgames. It wasn't until I was in college that it dawned on me that everyone, including Tiffany, was expecting us to get married. You know Tiffany. She's as helpless as a new-born kitten. How could I hurt her? The answer was, I couldn't. I decided it wouldn't be too bad; at least Tiffany always did whatever I wanted.' He grinned with derision at a sudden sound from Susan. 'I can tell that you aren't impressed with my knightly behaviour. No comment? Well, I suppose had things remained the same, Tiffany and I would have got married. I don't know that we would have been unhappy; bored, maybe. Fortunately for both Tiffany and me, Steve Tallerton showed up. He took one look at Tiffany and was a goner. I'm ashamed to say that I viewed Steve's infatuation as my salvation and did everything to aid and abet him. He was so honourable that he would have left without ever saying anything to Tiffany, but it was readily apparent to me that Tiffany returned his love, and I quickly convinced Steve of that fact.' He smiled in rueful memory. 'It was easier to convince him of that than to convince him to elope.'

'You mean it was your idea that they elope?' Susan squeaked.

'Can you imagine the turmoil if Tiffany had tried to tell her dad that she'd changed her mind? Tiffany would never have been able to face up to it. Running off was the only way.'

'But, but . . . if eloping was your idea, why did Tiffany feel so guilty about jilting you?'

Burke gave her a look of loving disgust. 'I could hardly tell Tiffany that I was jubilant about getting rid of her, could I? I drove her to the airport and managed to portray myself as someone who was giving her up to the better man, out of love, of course.'

'You fooled everyone.'

'Too well, I'm afraid. When Steve died, everyone immediately assumed that now Tiffany and I would get together again. Even Tiffany felt a sense of obligation, a sense that was sorely tried when she came out here last year and met her dad's new ranch manager. As for Neal, he fell like a ton of bricks. It was Steve all over again. At first, Tiffany was determined not to hurt me, so she didn't tell me about Neal, and I was more or less in despair that my choices were to go through with the marriage this time or hurt her badly in telling her that I wasn't interested. Meanwhile, half the county was taking bets on how soon the wedding would take place. Then you came along, and whatever else she is, Tiffany can be pretty shrewd sometimes. It took her about a minute and a half to see the whole picture, and realise that hurting me was the last thing she had to worry about. No, Neal was her problem. He refused to speak because he was the just the Senator's manager, while Tiffany was the boss's daughter. I understand that the successful conclusion of that courtship can be attributed to you.' He looked down at her, smiling with a whimsical twist of his firm lips.

'I didn't do anything.' The look on his face brought soft colour to her cheeks.

'You were like the chinook wind that blows down from the mountains in the spring, blowing everyone in your path off his course.'

'Is that a fancier way of saying you still think I'm a busybody?' Susan asked suspiciously.

'You have to admit you stirred things up! Tiffany and Neal got together. Randy, for the first time in his life, is thinking hard about his future because you convinced him he should decide it, not me. Even Elizabeth is considering moving to her own apartment.'

'Elizabeth is moving?'

'She said your drive and independence made her realise that she's just marking time down on the ranch. That there were things she could be doing to make herself count.'

As remarkable as Elizabeth's news was, Susan still hadn't heard that Burke was in any way affected by her visit. She fussed with the buttons on his shirt, refusing to meet his eyes. 'Lucky for you that you're too strong to be blown about by the wind.'

Burke laughed, a low sensuous laugh that set her pulse pounding. 'No, you didn't blow into my life. You crashed in.' Cradling her face between his hands, his voice vibrated with emotion as he added, 'When I saw you lying there, so still in your car, the world seemed to stop.'

'I notice it didn't render you speechless,' she said drily.

Burke grinned. 'You came out of that car, spitting fury, and it was all I could do not to grab you and kiss you until you shut up.'

'Why didn't you?' she teased.

'Are you kidding! You were icier than the weather.'

Saucily she stuck her tongue out at him. Moving like lightning, he reached down and gently grabbed the tip with his teeth. His lips touched hers, and all thoughts of Tiffany fled as he pressed open her mouth, his tongue tenderly bathing where his teeth had nipped. Tugging her head back to lie in the crook of his shoulder, one large hand encased her neck, his rough thumb caressing the pulse beat that his kisses accelerated. Willingly she accepted his gentle plundering of her mouth, giving a low cry of discontent when he abandoned its softness. Burke chuckled, and to punish him, she denied him her lips, hiding her face once again in his shoulder. She couldn't feel that he was properly chastised, however, when he began bestowing light nibbles on her exposed ear.

'Even when I was the angriest with you, I wanted to do that. I told myself that it was just a physical reaction to your loveliness, your fire. Your constant defiance and cockiness became a challenge to me.' He ignored her indignant gasp. 'You flaunted your independence, and my masculine ego couldn't take it. I wanted you. I wanted to make wild, abandoned love to you until you acknowledged my male authority. I wanted to dominate you.'

The blood pounded in Susan's temples at Burke's arrogant confession, and she could feel the bottom drop out of her world. All this talk was sexual. Burke didn't love her. She tried to escape his imprisoning grasp, but he held her easily. He hadn't finished.

'It wasn't until the Christmas tree that I realised that I had fallen in love with you.'

'In . . . in love?' she stammered.

'I knew then that I couldn't bear to live with a woman who would never disagree with me, who would accept my every whim, who would bore me to tears. Tiffany would have been horrified at Elizabeth's mugging, but she would have been too scared to give chase. But you . . .'

Susan shook her head. She couldn't let Burke make her into someone she was not. 'I *was* scared. In fact, I was terrified.'

Burke smoothed her damp hair away from her face. 'The point is that, regardless of the consequences, you did what you thought was right. Whether it was me or walking in the cold and dark the night you arrived, you always fought back. When you thought I was wrong, you stood up to me. And then, when I saw that silly tree, I knew that underneath your prickly exterior was a marshmallow heart. You can't bear to see someone hurt. Elizabeth, Randy, Ronnie, Tiffany—you tried to protect and help them all. I was jealous. I wanted you to care about me, too. The night we played cards, you would have let me make love to you then, and suddenly I realised that I wanted you to come to my bed out of desire, not out of generosity, and I couldn't be sure how you felt. Because by then, I realised that you thought it was Tiffany and me, and I knew you weren't the type to try and come between us. Tiffany was still working on Neal, and I couldn't give away her secret, not even to you. I knew she planned to announce their plans at the party, and I was counting on that night to be special for us, too.'

'The party.' Susan shuddered. 'You hated me for that.'

'I thought it was a dream come true. I couldn't believe that you felt the same as I did. Then I overheard you talking to Elizabeth. There you were, a mother hen protecting her chick. Thinking about all those loving looks, the constant possessive touches, and all fake, made me furious. I was just another sorry-looking Christmas tree that you were trying to convince everyone was beautiful.' He gave her a sheepish look. 'That old male ego again!'

Susan's eyes clouded with consternation. 'I wasn't feeling pity for you, Burke. It was—oh, I don't know. It just hurt me to think of you being hurt. But I couldn't explain that to you, not when you were acting like an outraged bull.'

Burke tilted her head up, forcing her to look at him. 'Can you ever forgive me for that night?.'

Susan chose her words very carefully. There could be no misunderstanding about what had happened. 'I thought you left me because at the last minute you couldn't bear the thought of me as a substitute for Tiffany.'

'My God, is that what you thought? No wonder you didn't want to see me tonight! Sweetheart, believe me, Tiffany was the last person in my thoughts that night.' He referred to her earlier accusation. 'Yes, I guess I was acting somewhat like an enraged bull. Rather than accept that you were concerned about me, I was determined to smash the pity I thought I saw on your face. My only thought was to force myself on you, to make you accept my male superiority and dominate you. Once and for all to make you admit that you were the weaker.'

'You must have thrilled with your success.'

A muscle clenched in his jaw. 'What success? I thought I wanted you cringing at my feet. I was wrong. When you refused to submit, and then I saw that tear on your face . . . all I wanted to do was comfort you. Then, when I would have apologised and left you, you responded with loving generosity, completely unmanning me.'

'So, thinking I'd won, you walked out on me.'

'Hell, by the time I got all your clothes off, I didn't care who won or lost, all I wanted was to take sweet possession.'

'Then I still don't understand why you walked out on me.'

'Laying you down on the bed, I got my first good look at you. Red marks on your shoulders and arms testified to the way I'd grabbed you. Your swollen lips . . . no loving kisses make a woman's lips bruised and bleeding like yours were. When I saw that, I just sort of went crazy. I had to get out of that room before I bawled like a baby at what I'd done.'

'But you said such awful things to me!'

'Did I? I don't even remember. I was so appalled at what I'd done, all I could think about was getting away from you before I hurt you more. I hated myself; what kind of contemptible swine forces himself on a woman?' A hesitant finger traced her lips. 'I've been haunted ever since you left by the memories of that night. That, and the thought of my own stupidity.'

'Stupidity?' Burke's fleeting touch, combined with his astounding confession, had shattered Susan's composure and she could barely think.

'Stupidity,' he reaffirmed. 'Here was the kind of woman my heart had been waiting for all my life, and I'd been too blind to realise it. A woman who would face life beside me, not hiding behind me. One who would laugh at life's adversities, and yet who could take the time to see the beauty in the small things. She'd been under my roof and in my bed. But it was too late for me. I'd sent her away.'

'You could have come after me.'

'After that night? Your only sin had been to treat me with compassion, and I brutalised you.'

Susan stirred uneasily. 'It wasn't that bad.'

'Bad enough,' said Burke grimly. 'You didn't like me before. There was no reason to think that my treating you violently made you think any better of me.'

'But I didn't dislike you.'

'So Elizabeth insisted.' He pressed a light kiss on her brow. 'I'd counted on seeing you at Tiffany's wedding. I thought I could get some clue as to my chances by how you behaved towards me. When you didn't show up, I was even more impossible to live with than before. Elizabeth finally blew her top. She said I'd better stop acting like a baby whose favourite toy had been stolen. I finally had to confess to her I'd muffed it with you.'

'You didn't tell her everything?' She'd never be able to face Elizabeth again.

Burke gave her a comforting squeeze. 'I left out a few details. She said that the look on your face the morning you left was so woebegone, she almost cried herself. I didn't really believe her then. But the more I considered the matter, the more I realised that, improbable as it seemed, you must love me or you never would have been willing to go to bed with me. It's taken me since then to get up the courage to come up here. Elizabeth told me that today was the last day of school before your spring vacation, so I was determined to come and have it out with you. While I waited for you to get home I sat out in the car and practised fancy speeches. Only you didn't show up. By the time you did I was frantic with worry.'

'Thus your loving greeting when I drove up.'

'You know the worst about me now. A terrible temper . . .'

'You can't stand to be crossed, and you jump to conclusions,' she finished for him.

'How was I to guess your brother was visiting you?'

'And you always blame me when it's your fault,' she said plaintively.

'Am I asking too much of you? I love you more than I could ever say, but I can't promise I won't shout at you and try to coerce you into giving me my own way. I'm a little domineering.'

Susan laughed softly. 'You're a lot domineering; you're arrogant, self-centred, and a chauvinist. If I marry you, you'll spend the rest of your life trying to bully me.'

'Are you brave enough to take on a proposition like that? It's a life-time sentence. I won't consider anything shorter.'

'In the interests of preventing some other poor

female from falling under your thumb, I don't think I have any choice.'

'No choice at all,' Burke agreed, his head blotting out the rest of the room as he lowered his lips to hers.

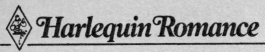

Coming Next Month

2881   DREAM OF LOVE   Kay Clifford
Posing as her film star boss's fiancée, Melissa accompanies him to
California. It is a position she finds difficult to explain when she
meets and falls in love with another man!

2882   NIGHT OF THE SPRING MOON   Virginia Hart
A young woman who returns to her Missouri hometown—and to
the man she once loved—finds herself in an emotional dilemma.
She's torn between her renewed feelings for him and loyalty to her
best friend.

2883   HIGH COUNTRY GOVERNESS   Essie Summers
Sheer desperation drives New Zealand sheep station owner
Nathanial Pengelly to hire the head beautician from his father's
store as a governess. But Letty is far more than just a lovely face and
sets out to teach him an unforgettable lesson!

2884   HIDDEN DEPTHS   Nicola West
Tessa doesn't expect open arms when she arrives in Arizona to
bridge years of silence between her mother and her grandfather.
But at least she intends to see him. If only her arrogant cousin will
stop acting as guardian gatekeeper!

2885   BITTER DECEPTION   Gwen Westwood
Journalist Sophia, visiting the cottage she's inherited in France,
finds her neighbor, famous mountain climber Fabien de Cressac,
accessible and irresistible—so she interviews him. As love grows
between them, however, she realizes the published story will end
their relationship....

2886   TO TAME A WILD HEART   Quinn Wilder
Guide Chance Cody has no use for spoiled rich brats—especially
Aurora Fairhurst who's joined his wilderness trek to escape an
arranged marriage. Not until Aurora finds a new honest self, does
she find the way to his heart.

Available in January wherever paperback books are sold, or
through Harlequin Reader Service.

In the U.S.
901 Fuhrmann Blvd.
P.O. Box 1397
Buffalo, N.Y. 14240-1397

In Canada
P.O. Box 603
Fort Erie, Ontario
L2A 5X3

For the millions who can't read
Give the Gift of Literacy

One out of five adults in North America
cannot read or write well enough
to fill out a job application
or understand the directions on a bottle of medicine.

**You can change all this by joining the fight
against illiteracy.**

For more information write to:
Contact, Box 81826, Lincoln, Neb. 68501
In the United States, call toll free: 1-800-228-8813

**The only degree you need
is a degree of caring**

LIT-A-1R